8 Weeks

Time for Love Series

Book 1

By
Bethany Lopez

Susan,
True love always
wins! ♡

Bethany Lopez
AAD 2014

Visit the author's website:
www.bethanylopez.blogspot.com

Books by Bethany Lopez

Young Adult:

Stories about Melissa – series
Ta Ta for Now!
xoxoxo
Ciao
TTYL

Nissa: a contemporary fairy tale

New Adult:

Friends & Lovers Trilogy
Make it Last
I Choose You
Trust in Me

Indelible

A Time for Love Series
8 Weeks

This book is dedicated to the men and women that I've served with in the Air Force over the years... It's been quite a ride!

Chapter 1 – Cal

I lifted my throbbing head from the mattress and glanced around the blurry room. Nothing looked familiar. I closed my eyes tightly and reopened them, hoping to bring the room into focus and discover where I was. Closing my eyes relieved some of the pain, but as soon as I opened them again, the bright morning light felt like a laser searing my skull.

"Fuck!" I raised myself up gingerly, on shaky arms, as the night before came back to me in fits and glimpses.

I was in Vegas.

We'd had my buddy's bachelor party the night before.

I'd gotten completely fuckin' wasted.

I was able to get into a sitting position, bringing my elbows up to rest on my knees, and cradle my head in my hands. I peered down around my palms and got an eyeful of my junk.

I was butt-ass naked.

What the fuck had happened last night? I closed my eyes tightly and tried to remember, but it was no use. When my stomach began turn, I heaved myself off of the bed and looked around for a place to vomit. I had no idea where the bathroom was, but was able to make it to the trashcan by the desk before the puke flew past my lips. A moan escaped my lips as my stomach cramped and some remnants of last night's dinner came out of my mouth and nose simultaneously.

The retching went on for a few minutes. My nose burned and there was a chunk of something lodged in the back of my throat.

Stomach empty, I sat back on my heels and wiped my mouth with the back of my hand. Now not only was my head pounding like a drum, but my mouth tasted like I'd been licking the ass-end of a horse for the better part of the morning.

I curled into a ball on the floor by the trashcan, willing the room to be still, so my stomach would stop twirling violently. It was no use. I felt the bile begin to rise and got up quickly to hug the trashcan again, hurling and heaving until there was nothing left but the foam from the pit of my stomach.

The sound of a flush, then water running had me turning my head toward what must've been the bathroom. A few seconds later, the door opened and a statuesque blonde strode out and picked up her dress from the back of a chair. She turned to me, naked as I was, and shook her head with a chuckle.

"That was some party," she said as she pulled the dress over her head and walked toward the door. When her hand touched the handle she turned back to me and smiled. "Have a nice life, sugar." Then she walked out, the door slamming behind her.

I sat there for a moment. Speechless, naked, reeking of alcohol and puke.

"No, no, no, no, no, no …" I muttered as I began to rock back and forth on my heels. This couldn't be happening to me.

Where were the guys?

How had I gotten back to this room?

What the fuck had I done, and how was I ever going to explain this to my wife?

Chapter 2 – Shelly

As I finished cutting up vegetables for the salad, I looked around the kitchen and into the dining room to see if I'd forgotten anything. Table set and made beautiful with tulips and candlesticks in cheerful shades of yellow, roast cooking in the oven, and shrimp sautéing in a pan on top of the stove for an appetizer. Everything looked, and smelled, wonderful.

I smiled happily as I hummed to myself, excited to surprise Cal when he got home from his "boy's trip" to Vegas.

It was our sixth wedding anniversary, and I couldn't wait for him to see my new dress. It was a little white dress that hugged my curves in all the right places.

When we'd gotten married at eighteen, right out of high school, everyone said we'd never last. But I'd known from the second I'd laid eyes on Cal at a pep rally our junior year of high school that he was the man I wanted to be with for the rest of my life. He'd been making me happy every day since.

I took the salad bowl to the table, complete with the moose-shaped salad tongs that Cal had bought me on our cruise to Alaska, and placed it in the center of the table. I straightened the wine goblets with our initials that Cal had brought home as a surprise for me when I'd gotten promoted to manager at the bank.

I could look all around our sweet little house and bask in the memories we'd made so far.

I turned off the stovetop and covered the pan, then ran to the back of the house to our bathroom. Checking myself in the mirror, I was happy to see that my hair and makeup were holding up. I turned and walked into our bedroom, taking off clothes as I moved. I had my outfit laid out on the bed, down to the white garter belt and stockings. I took care putting on the underthings, so as not to get a snag and ruin the sexy little treat I had just bought for Cal. I looked in the full-length mirror as I slipped the dress over my head, then turned around, checking to make sure everything was in its proper place.

With my dark hair in soft waves and my ruby red lips contrasting the stark white of my outfit, I realized the last time I'd felt this sexy and beautiful was on our wedding day.

Cal was going to be so turned on, I thought with a giggle, the blush on my cheeks only accentuating the look I was going for.

The beeping of the oven timer sounded off in the kitchen and I nodded at myself in the mirror before returning to the kitchen.

The night was going to be perfect.

I pulled the roast out, leaving it covered as I sat it on the counter so the flavors could come together. I went to the small wine rack, my first purchase when we bought this house, our first home, and pulled our favorite bottle of red. I opened it swiftly, then set it on the counter to breathe.

I looked around again, mentally checking items off the list in my head as I surveyed the rooms. One of the selling points of this house for me had been the open floor plan. I loved the way the rooms opened up to each other, really giving the house a homey feel.

Realizing I'd forgotten to freshen up my deodorant, I ran back through the house, checking the clock on the wall and squealing when I realized that Cal should be home any minute. I quickly put on deodorant, sprayed Cal's favorite perfume, and slipped on a pair of sling back heels.

At six foot four, Cal towered over my five-foot-six frame. I loved it. Being in his arms always made me feel feminine and safe.

As I was walking down the hall, I heard the sound of the garage door going up, and my stomach dipped in anticipation of Cal's arrival. I put on my brightest smile and positioned myself seductively against the counter, so I would be the first thing he saw when he walked through the door.

Chapter 3 - Cal

I sat in my car in the garage for a few minutes, terrified of going inside and facing Shelly. As soon as she saw me, she would know something was wrong. She had a knack for reading me. She always had.

The guys had stumbled in a few minutes after the blonde turned my world upside down.

"Jesus," my buddy Scott, whose pending nuptials we were in Vegas celebrating, said as he made out my naked, vomit-covered form. "What the fuck happened to you?"

"Where were you guys?" I asked bleakly, trying to pull myself into a sitting position.

"Well, after you said you were heading back here, pussy that you are, we continued our little party. We hit up a club at the Hard Rock, then went out for breakfast. We haven't slept yet." This was said in a mind-numbing tone by my other buddy, TJ.

"Have you been like this all night?" Scott

asked.

I put my head in my hands and tried to control my shaking body.

"I really fucked up," I said.

"Dude," TJ said, throwing my jeans at me. "Put some pants on. I can't listen to you when your junk is on display."

I leaned back and tried to wiggle into my jeans without disturbing my stomach. Once I was dressed, I filled them in on my morning.

Scott and TJ were staring at me, horrified. Scott started pacing the floor and asked, "Do you remember where you met her or how you got back here?"

"No. I don't remember a fucking thing," I admitted.

"Maybe nothing happened," TJ said hopefully.

"We were both naked, and although I don't remember the details, I'm pretty sure we had sex."

"Shit," Scott muttered. "What are you going to do?"

"What do you mean?" I asked miserably. "I have to tell Shelly the truth."

"Are you sure that's a good idea, man? She'll never hear it from us," TJ said. Scott nodded his agreement.

"I can't do that. I can't lie to her."

"It's either lie to her, or break her heart, Cal," Scott said with a frown.

Scott and TJ had been my best friends since middle school. They'd been with me at the pep rally when I'd first laid eyes on Shelly and they stood up in my wedding.

The trip back had been long and torturous as I tried to figure out what I should do. Shelly and I had a great relationship and I'd never lied to her. I didn't want to start now, but what Scott said was true. It would break her heart, and I knew our relationship would never be the same, but I also knew that I wouldn't be able to live with this lie for the rest of our lives.

Quit being a bitch and go inside, I said to myself, trying to talk myself into getting out of the car.

I really didn't want to, but I knew that she'd probably heard the garage door, and would be waiting for me to come inside.

Fuck.

I grabbed my overnight bag and reluctantly opened the car door.

When I opened the door and saw Shelly leaning against the counter in the sexiest little dress I'd ever seen, I wanted to rewind the last couple days and not go on the Vegas trip.

I looked around the room, noted the candles, flowers, and the sweet smell of my favorite dinner on the stove, and felt like I'd just been punched in the gut.

It was our anniversary.

I'd been so wrapped up in my misery, I'd forgotten. I had a gift that I'd bought a few days ago for her in the closet. Man, that seemed like ages ago.

My face must have betrayed my despair, because Shelly pushed off the counter and came to me, her hands coming up to immediately cup my face.

"What's wrong?" She asked.

I closed my eyes briefly and breathed in the sweet smell of her. I pulled her into my arms and held on tightly, knowing that in a few minutes, she wasn't going to want me to touch her.

I wished momentarily that I could lie to her. That I could just forget what happened and enjoy my wife and our anniversary, but I knew I'd never be able to live with myself. So I allowed myself the comfort of her body and kissed her lips softly before pulling away and saying, "Oh, baby, I'm so sorry."

Chapter 4 – Shelly

It's crazy how much things can change in an instant.

One moment, I was eagerly awaiting my husband's arrival. I was feeling excited and sexy, and anticipating an evening filled with love and great sex.

Then, with a few words, my whole world came crashing down around me, and my life changed.

I went from being a whole person, to having my heart shattered into a million fragmented pieces.

I was looking into my handsome man's face, my lips still tingling from his kiss, when he started to apologize.

I'd known something was up when he walked in, but I'd never imagined the depths of what was wrong.

"Sorry about what?" I asked tentatively,

unsure if I wanted to know the answer.

"Let's go sit down," Cal said, but I shook my head.

"Just say it."

"I don't remember what happened last night, apparently I got really drunk and left the guys in the casino and headed back to the room. The last thing I remember is them razzing me about being a lightweight." I smiled at him; he'd always been kind of a lightweight. The look on his face caused the smile to fall from mine. "When I woke up this morning, I was naked with a killer hangover, and there was someone else in the room."

"One of the guys?" I asked, suddenly filled with dread.

Cal shook his head slowly, and my arms dropped from around him. I stepped back, the look in his eyes telling me what he was going to say before he said it.

I shook my head in denial.

"It was a woman," he said softly, his voice strained. "I don't know who she was or how I met her, but I'm pretty sure I slept with her."

"No," I replied sharply. "You wouldn't do that."

Cal brought his arms up as if to touch me and I stepped back farther. He dropped his arms sadly and responded, "I know. I wouldn't consciously sleep with someone else; you're the only one for me, Shel, but I was so messed up …"

A hot ball of tears began to form in my throat and I turned on my heels, walking back toward the bedroom.

I had to get out of there.

I walked into my closet and pulled my backpack down from the shelf. I was stuffing clothes into it when Cal came into the room.

"What are you doing?" he asked, his voice filled with desperation.

"Going to my dad's," I said stiffly.

"Shelly, we need to talk about this."

I stopped what I was doing and glared at him. "What is there to talk about? You *cheated* on me. On us."

"I know, baby, but I didn't know what I was doing. You have to believe me."

"Is that supposed to make it okay?" I asked, tears falling freely down my cheeks. I had the sudden urge to punch him in the face.

"No, of course not, but you can't just walk out. We need to talk this through."

I zipped my backpack and threw it over my shoulder, then walked purposefully past him and out toward the garage.

"Shelly," Cal called out.

When his hand touched my arm, I yanked it away and said, "Don't touch me."

He held up his hands as if in surrender and said, "Please ... Don't go. Don't do this."

"I didn't do anything, you did. I can't stay," I sobbed. "I can't stand to look at you."

I turned my back on the hurt look on his face and slammed the door on my way out.

I got into my little Ford pickup and peeled out in the driveway in my haste to get as far away from Cal as possible. As I drove on autopilot, the enormity of the situation weighed heavily on my mind.

The only man I'd ever loved, who I'd always trusted implicitly, had just made a mockery of everything I'd thought and felt over the last six years of our relationship.

I was in shock.

I'd always believed that Cal and I would be together forever ... That we'd have children and grow old together.

That he would never hurt me.

Well, he hadn't just hurt me. He'd crushed me. He'd crushed *us*.

I pulled up to the home I'd grown up in and had barely turned off the car before I was catapulting out of it. I ran up the steps and put my key in the door. I flung it open, sobbing and crying, and looked around frantically.

My dad came out of the kitchen, his face covered in surprise as he looked at me. I was still in my anniversary outfit and must have looked half out of my mind.

I was.

"Shell Bell, what's going on? Are you hurt?"

"Oh, Daddy," I cried as I rushed into his arms and held on tightly.

He patted my back and murmured that everything would be okay. And although I knew that this was one thing my father wouldn't be able to fix for me, I allowed myself to be soothed by his words.

Chapter 5 – Cal

I dropped to my knees after she walked out the door. I'm not sure how long I stayed there, staring at the closed door, willing it to open again and to have Shelly walk back in. It never did.

When I got up and walked around the dining room, followed by the kitchen, my stomach clenched at the effort she'd put into the evening. I could feel the love and happiness that had gone into the planning and execution of our anniversary celebration, and it killed me that I'd ruined all of it.

I walked back to our bedroom and sat on the bed. As I stared at Shelly's open drawers, I grabbed my cell phone out of my pocket and dialed Scott.

"'Lo," he said after one ring.

"She left," I said simply.

"I'm on my way," Scott said. I could hear his keys jingling as he hung up the phone.

Scott had been my best friend since the

moment we both rode up on our Huffy bikes on the first day of sixth grade. We could count on each other in good times and bad, and he was the only person other than Shelly that I could go to when I needed to talk.

I thought about the look on her face when she realized what I was about to confess. I never wanted to put that look on her face, and I was torn apart that I had.

The first time I saw Shelly, my initial thoughts were not of marriage. I was sixteen years old, and she was the prettiest girl I'd ever seen. Her green eyes made her entire face light up, her long brown hair had been pulled back into a ponytail, and her body was to die for. I wanted her. Badly. It was that simple.

"Dibs," I'd called out to Scott and TJ when I saw her. They'd both followed my gaze and TJ'd replied, "Shit … She's fine."

I don't know where I'd gotten the courage, but I walked right up to her and started talking. I'd asked her out for that weekend, and she'd said yes. We'd been together ever since, and I'd never wanted anyone else. This was why I found it unfathomable, that no matter how wasted I was, I would've cheated on her. I just couldn't believe it.

"Cal," Scott yelled from somewhere in the

house.

"Back here," I responded.

"Dude, what's up with the spread?" Scott asked as he walked in.

"It's our six-year wedding anniversary," I responded miserably.

"Fuck. I forgot."

I nodded, then looked up at him and repeated what I'd told him earlier on the phone. "She left. She wouldn't stay and talk about it."

"Bro, I'm so sorry. I'm sure she's hurt right now. Give her some space, and then explain everything. Beg. Grovel. Whatever you have to do. It's you and Shel, man, you'll work it out."

"You think?" I asked, hopeful.

But he hadn't seen how I'd crushed her.

I shook my head.

"I don't know. It's a pretty unforgivable thing."

"Hey, if anyone can get past this, it's you guys. Just give her some time and then do whatever you have to do to make it right."

"I don't want to be here," I said, looking around our bedroom. Shelly had taken such care to make our home special, and there were reminders of us everywhere.

"C'mon," Scott said, gesturing toward the

door. "You can crash at my place as long as you want."

"Thanks, man," I said as I rose from the bed.

I grabbed a pair of jeans and a shirt, along with my work clothes, and threw them in a bag, then I went into the bathroom and got what I'd need for a couple days.

When I walked into the kitchen, Scott was putting everything away.

"What are you doing?" I asked.

"Just trying to help out. I didn't want either of you to have to come home to a mess that would remind you of today."

That's why he was my best friend. I could always fucking count on him.

"Thanks, man." I clapped him on the back, then started clearing the table.

We were done a few minutes later and headed out the door. I followed him in my Mustang, since I'd need it to get to work in the morning.

I worked in a garage with TJ; we had worked there since our senior year of high school. Neither of us were the type of guys to go to college and get some big business job; we left that to Scott. We were more than happy to be turning wrenches and coming home dirty every night.

I loved the feeling of fixing something that

was thought to be broken. I even enjoyed the mundane tasks, like changing oil and rotating tires.

Shelly had always been proud of my work, just like I was proud of her work at the bank. We were happy. At least we *were*. Now I didn't know what was going to happen, and that scared me.

Our future had always seemed predestined. We met in high school, got married, and focused on our work and our life together. Now that we were both pretty established at our jobs, we had been talking about starting a family. It was perfect.

I felt lost, and not just a little afraid. I couldn't imagine a future without Shelly in it. I didn't want to.

I knew that I had to do whatever I possibly could to get her back. She had to listen to me, and she had to forgive me. There just wasn't any other alternative.

We were meant to be together.

Chapter 6 – Shelly

I cried for two days. I called in sick to work, turned off my cell phone, and hid out in my childhood bedroom. I just kept hearing him over and over in my head, "I'm pretty sure I slept with her."

How can you be "pretty sure"?

By the time the two days were over, it no longer mattered to me. All that mattered was that Cal slept with someone else.

He was not the man I thought he was.

My first order of business was to take a shower. I reeked.

Once I was scrubbed, shaved, and squeaky clean, I went out into the house in search of food. My dad was sitting at the kitchen table, reading the paper and drinking tea. Judging by the darkness outside, it was nighttime. I looked at the clock and was surprised to see it was eleven o'clock.

"What are you doing up?" I asked my dad as I

opened the refrigerator door.

"Hey, Bell," he said, grinning at me from around the paper. "It's good to see you up."

"It's late, why are you up?" I asked again.

"I figured you'd have to get up eventually, and I wanted to be here in case you needed to talk."

I put the carton of eggs on the counter, then walked over and kissed him on the head.

"That's sweet, Dad, but you should get some sleep."

"Nah, I'm retired. I can sleep whenever I want."

"Alright, do you want some eggs?" I asked.

"No, I already ate," he responded.

He continued to read his paper as I made my eggs, and I found his presence comforting.

When I sat down at the table next to him he said, "Cal's called a few times."

"I don't want to talk to him right now," I spat out. Just the sound of his name made me lose my appetite.

"That's what I told him," my dad replied. "Gaby and Sasha have also called a few times, I guess Cal told them you were here. They were worried because they haven't been able to get a hold of you."

"I turned my phone off," I explained as I pushed the eggs around on my plate.

"Well, you should give them a call, let 'em know you're okay."

I nodded. Sasha and Gaby were probably exactly what I needed right now. Great friends.

"You need to eat those eggs, not just play with them."

"I'll try," I said softly.

My dad stood up and gathered up his empty cup, then he kissed me on the head, mimicking my earlier gesture.

"You'll get through this, sweetheart. You're a strong woman, just like your mother."

"Thanks, Dad. Goodnight."

I sat there staring at the plate in front of me, wondering what I was going to do. I guessed that I'd have to go back to work; now was not the time to get fired. Plus, I needed to start thinking about money. Cal and I had always kept our money together and paid our bills. Now, we'd have to decide who was going to get the house and pay the bills, and divvy everything up. I was always the one who paid the bills, so Cal was going to have to start worrying about that on his own now.

I'd already decided that we would have to get a divorce. There's no way I'd be able to stay with him after what he did.

I picked up my plate and threw out my

uneaten food, then went to find my phone.

When I turned it on, there were numerous missed calls and text messages from Cal, Gaby, and Sasha. I ignored Cal's and went right to Gaby's. She started off worried, then pissed, and her final message simply said, *Call Me Now*.

I called her.

"Hello," Gaby said sleepily.

"Hey," I responded. "Did I wake you?"

"Shelly? You at your dad's?" she asked, a little more alert.

"Yeah."

"I'm coming over," Gaby said. Then she hung up.

"Hello?" I asked, but she was already gone.

I shouldn't have been surprised though, the three of us had always been like that. We could count on each other no matter what.

Gaby and I had been friends since elementary school. In fact, I couldn't remember a time in my life without her in it.

Sasha had moved into town our freshman year in high school. She'd been gorgeous, fashionable, and scared the shit out of everyone, so the majority of the school had shunned her almost immediately. Not ones to conform to the masses, Gaby and I had asked Sasha to sit with us during lunch ... We'd been inseparable ever since.

I was sitting on the couch, looking out the window, so I saw Gaby's VW Bug pull up in front of the house and got up to open the door for her.

She jogged up the path, into the house, and put her hands on my shoulders, looking me over everywhere.

"What the *fuck* is going on?" she asked finally.

I pulled her inside and shut the door, leaning against it as I answered her. When I finished telling her about Cal, her mouth was hanging wide open and she was shaking her head back and forth.

"No ... No, way. Not Cal, he loves you too much."

"Apparently not," I said with a bitter laugh. "He was drunk and doesn't remember, but it happened."

"What are you going to do?"

"I'm doing it, Gaby. I left him."

"But, he didn't do it on *purpose* ..." she began, then stopped when I shot her a glare.

"Don't you dare defend him."

"I'm not defending him, Shelly, but it's Cal. It's the two of you. You love each other and there's no way that he would have consciously went out and slept with another woman. You have to know that."

"I may know that, Gaby, but I also know that I

can't get the image of him with another woman out of my head. I can't stop thinking that he had sex with someone other than me," I explained as I paced the living room. "We were both each other's first and only lovers. That's not the case anymore, and I can't get it out of my head."

"Maybe with a little time you will," Gaby said softly.

"Please, stop. I know that you love both of us, Gaby, but I need you to be on my side on this," I pleaded.

"I'm always on your side, Shelly," Gaby promised. "No matter what."

Chapter 7 – Cal

"I'm going to do whatever it takes to get her back, man," I was explaining to TJ as I finished up with an oil change on a Charger.

"Dude, I really don't get what she's getting all freaked out about … I mean, I get it … but, it's not like you're having an affair or something. It was an honest mistake," TJ was saying as he organized his tools. He was anal about his toolboxes.

I stopped and gave him a look, "Are you being serious, TJ? It is a big deal. I fucked up majorly."

"All I'm saying is that you didn't plan it. It's not like when we hopped on the plane to Vegas you said, 'I'm getting me some strange this weekend.' Shelly will come around."

"I hope you're right, because as it stands now, she won't take any of my calls or answer any of my texts."

I heard the clicking of heels before the yelling began.

"You mother-fucking son-of-a-bitch!"

Great, just what I needed.

I turned and said, "Hey, Sasha," just as she rounded the corner.

Sasha was impressive even when she wasn't seething in anger. At about five foot nine with waves of red hair and legs that were a mile long, Sasha made an impression wherever she went.

"Don't you 'Hey' me, you low life. I just heard what you did to Shelly and I came straight here to kick your ass!"

"Did you talk to her?" I asked, brushing my hands on a rag as I walked toward her. I couldn't keep the worry out of my voice. "How's she doing?"

Sasha stopped a few feet away and tilted her head, her look puzzled.

"No, I didn't talk to her, but Gaby has. What's going on? Did you really cheat on her?" Some of the fight had gone out of her face, and she looked almost as sad as I felt.

I had to get away before I did something embarrassing, like break down.

"Not now, Sasha," I said with my hands up, before I turned and walked to the back of the shop.

The door didn't close all the way, so I could

hear TJ say to her, "He's having a hard time too, Sash, and he doesn't need you coming in here and bustin' his balls."

I could just imagine Sasha's face going from concerned right back to riled up. She and TJ had never been able to get along, but they both loved Shelly and me, so they usually made an attempt to.

"I didn't ask you, of course you're going to stick up for him, no matter what he's done."

"It's not like that. You know Cal would never do anything to hurt Shelly. The two of them are like a fifty-year-old married couple. He made a mistake. She's pissed. They'll work it out ... And they don't need you making it harder by getting all 'Amazon Woman' on Cal."

"Suck it, TJ," Sasha said, but her voice sounded less angry.

"What'd you do, hear about it at the coffee house or something and come storming over without getting the facts? You know Cal better than that. Why don't you cut him some slack and give him the benefit of the doubt. He's broken up about what happened. Give him a chance to make it right."

By Sasha's silence, I knew he was probably pretty accurate. Sasha was well known for her temper, especially when it came to her girls.

"Shit ... You're right. You know you'd react

the same way if the shoe was on the other foot. Tell Cal I'm sorry ... For now. But if I go and hear the same shit from Shelly that I heard at breakfast I'll be back."

"We wouldn't expect any less," TJ said, and I could hear the smirk in his voice.

I gave it a few minutes, until I was sure that I'd be able to hold my shit, then I walked outside.

"Is it safe?" I tried to lighten the mood a bit, although I felt anything but light.

"Yeah," TJ said with a grin. "She sure is hot when she's pissed though, huh?"

I chuckled at him. As much as they always got under each other's skin, I was surprised they'd never hooked up. It was a long-running joke in our group.

The thought of our group being fractured now was another stab to my heart. I'd fucked up more than I thought in one night. And I couldn't even remember why.

"I'm gonna go see Shelly," I said suddenly. "Can you cover for me here?"

TJ opened his arms and gestured around the empty bays.

"I think I can handle it."

"Thanks, brother."

I hopped in my Mustang and drove down to Shelly's dad's house. I knew my way well, I'd spent the last two years of high school driving there as much as possible. Her dad and I had always gotten along well, but by the sound of his voice when I'd tried calling, our days of being pals were over.

I pulled up to the house and looked at it for a minute before getting out, trying to regain the courage I'd had back at the shop. Now that I was here, I was terrified that she still wouldn't see me.

When I got to the door, I knocked softly and waited, straining to hear if there were any sounds coming from inside the house.

"You probably have to knock loud enough for her to hear you, jackass," I muttered to myself before closing my eyes, taking a deep breath, and knocking again. Louder this time.

I braced myself when the door started to open, and held my breath as I waited to see if it was going to be Shelly or her dad at the door.

"Hey," Shelly said softly when she'd opened the door a crack. "What are you doing here?"

I let out the breath I'd been holding and said, "We need to talk, Shelly."

"I don't want to talk right now, Cal."

"Shell, how will we ever work this out if you won't even talk to me?"

"There's nothing to work out."

"Nothing to work out?" I ran my hand

through my hair, frustrated, and turned back toward the street so I could breathe for a minute. She looked so upset, I couldn't stand it.

Once I was composed I turned back to her, "What do you mean, Shelly? We have a lot to work out."

She shook her head sadly at me.

"We have nothing that *can* be worked out, Cal."

I felt panic begin to rise in my throat, until I was in danger of choking on it.

"I don't understand."

"I want a divorce, Cal, and I'll let you know when I'm ready to talk about it."

She shut the door slowly in my face, as I stood there, stunned and speechless, with my life flashing before my eyes.

"No …" I whispered, unable to believe what she'd just said. I pounded on the door for a few minutes, desperate for her to come back and talk this out, but she never did.

Chapter 8 – Shelly

God, would I ever stop crying?

After I left Cal standing at my dad's front door, I climbed into the shower and let the water run over me as I cried my heart out.

I couldn't see any way to forgive Cal and stay married to him. I just couldn't. And, as much as it seemed impossible to do, I knew that I was going to have to pick myself up and figure out what my life looked like without him in it.

After a few more days of moping around, I finally agreed to meet the girls for lunch.

Sasha was in real estate, and Gaby worked at a bakery nearby the restaurant we were meeting at, so lunch was usually the best time to get together. We wouldn't have a ton of time, but a little time with the girls was better than none at all.

I took some time to make myself look presentable. I'd lost a few pounds over the last couple weeks, and I had to put my makeup on a little heavier to cover the circles under my eyes.

When I got to the restaurant, Gaby was already there, drinking what I'd bet was a diet coke and talking to a waiter. He was tall, dark, and really good-looking and she blushed slightly when she saw me walking toward the table.

"Hey, Gabs," I said as I leaned down to kiss her cheek.

"What was that about?"

"Oh, nothing," Gaby said with a wave of her hand. "He was just asking me out for coffee."

"Oooh, really?" I said, happy to be talking about something normal. Every guy who came in to contact with Gaby asked her out. But, she usually said the same thing. "So, what'd you say?"

"No, thanks, but maybe another time," she responded with a smile.

"I wish you'd say yes one of these days," I admitted.

"I will," Gaby replied. "When it feels right."

Gaby seemed to be able to read men better than anyone I'd ever met. She was like the man-whisperer. She always seemed to know if a guy was good for her or not, and she was always very choosy about who she dated. She'd had two boyfriends since I'd known her, and they'd both been relationships that lasted over two years.

Gaby did not do casual relationships, much to every man within a sixty-mile radius's disappointment.

I heard the heels before the whirlwind hit, and I knew Sasha had made it.

Sasha, on the other hand, *loved* casual relationships.

Sasha loved to buy expensive things and pamper herself consistently, and was very focused on her career. She didn't want a man in her life who thought he would get to have a say in what she did and how she did it, so she always kept them at arm's length. She used them for sex and arm candy, and that was about it.

My friends and I were all completely different, but we loved each other unconditionally. We were lucky that it had always been that way. There had been people that tried to come between us, male and female, but no one was ever able to break that bond.

One of the things I'd loved about Cal was that he'd always gotten it. My friendship with my girls … because he had the same thing with his friends.

Shit … Cal.

I felt the sadness creeping in again, until Sasha grabbed my chin, looked me in the eye, and said, "Nuh-uh, girlfriend. Chin up."

I smiled shakily at her, and tried to nod. But it was difficult, since she was still holding my chin. She chuckled and released me.

"How are you?" Sasha whispered.

I sighed deeply and said, "Crushed."

"Oh, baby, I'm so sorry."

Sasha pulled me tightly to her and I held on as if I were afraid to let go. She smelled of perfume and hair product, and I found it very soothing.

"Do you want me to put a hit out on him?" Sasha asked seriously.

I chuckled and replied, "Not today."

Gaby leaned across the table and asked, "Have you talked to him?"

I shook my head.

"I haven't been able to. I can't look at him right now. He stopped by the other day, and I saw him long enough to tell him I want a divorce, then I ran back inside."

Gaby gasped at my statement.

"Are you sure that's what you want, Shelly? Don't you want to talk it over with him first, maybe think about it for a while?"

I shook my head and felt tears forming.

"I don't think it'll make a difference. He betrayed me in a way that I never believed was possible." They each took one of my hands in theirs as I spoke. "I think I need a clean break, and I need to start figuring out what to do with my life."

"Let us know what you need," Sasha said.

I turned to Sasha and said, "I want to sell the house."

"Are you sure?"

"Yeah, neither of us will be able to afford it on our own, and I need to start fresh. I'd like to rent something for now, an apartment or condo or something."

"Okay, but you will have to discuss this with Cal and come to an agreement. The house is in both of your names."

I nodded. I knew I'd have to talk with him eventually. I was just really not looking forward to it.

We paused our conversation and ordered lunch from the dark-haired waiter who kept looking at Gaby longingly.

"Gaby, dude's got a fine ass," Sasha said with a wicked grin as she watched him walk away. "You should take him around back and give him what he's asking for."

"Shut up, Sasha," Gaby said with a laugh.

I laughed with my friends and knew I wanted to spend more time with them, so I wasn't miserable and alone at my dad's.

"We should do something Friday night," I

said.

"I'm free, what did you have in mind?" Sasha asked.

"I don't know ... something different. Something I'd never do with Cal," I said the wheels in my head turning. "I've always wanted to get a tattoo, get my nose pierced, and I've been thinking of cutting my hair."

"Slow down, sister," Gaby stopped me before I could throw out any other ideas. "How about we do one crazy, body-altering thing at a time. We wouldn't want you to do something that you'd regret to get back at Cal."

I frowned at her.

"I don't want to do any of it to get back at Cal, I want to do it for myself. Those are things that I've always wanted to do, I just didn't think he'd approve. It's about my independence, and the fact that I don't need Cal's approval anymore."

"Well, when you put it that way, I'm all in," Sasha said loudly, causing the other patrons to turn and look at us.

"Okay, well, how about we start with the piercing, then go out for drinks and show it off?" Gaby said in a softer tone.

"Sounds good," I said, clasping my hands together nervously. It would be good to get out and stop moping around, but I was a little nervous at the same time. I tried to put on a brave face and said, "I'm excited."

"In the meantime, you need to sit down and talk to Cal," she said sternly.

I nodded sadly, "I know."

Chapter 9 – Cal

I was on my way to meet with Shelly. My palms were sweating and my stomach was rolling. I'd never been so nervous in my life.

I'd been a wreck since the last time I'd seen her.

I couldn't believe she was talking about a divorce; it was the last thing in the world I wanted. Shelly was everything to me, and I couldn't imagine my life without her.

I was so messed up, I worried that Scott was on the verge of kicking me out. He said he was tired of my stinky, miserable ass, permanently indented on his couch. I knew he was fuckin' with me, but he had a point. I needed to get my shit together if I ever even hoped to get Shelly back.

I had to come up with a plan. A plan to make her give me a chance to make up for the mistake I'd made. There had to be a way that we could get past this and heal.

Yes, on paper it seemed unforgivable.

But … I had to believe that she could. She'd always been it for me, and nothing was more important than keeping her as my wife.

I pulled up to the park Shelly'd told me to meet her at. She'd wanted to meet somewhere public, but without a lot of people around.

I was pretty upset that she seemed to distrust me on every level, but understood that she was hurt.

I would be too, if it were the other way around.

I saw her sitting at a picnic table under a giant oak with leaves of copper, red, and a deep russet, her long dark hair wavy and flowing in the breeze. The picture she made took my breath away, and I stood there, committing it to memory, before I walked forward to meet her.

"Hey," I said as I got closer, causing her to jump a bit on the bench.

She looked up at me warily, and I felt that look punch me in the gut.

I had the feeling she was not here to tell she was ready to give us another shot. I was going to have to buy myself some time.

"Hi," Shelly responded.

I sat down across from her and folded my

hands in front of me. I was nervous and felt awkward. Two things I'd never been around Shelly in my life. Even when we started dating.

"So," she began, then stopped, clearing her throat nervously. "There's no easy way to say this, so I'm just going to say it … I've been thinking, and we need to put the house on the market as soon as possible. You never know how long it'll take to sell, and neither of us make the kind of money that would allow us to pay for two houses at once."

"What the hell are you talking about?" I asked, anger and hurt mingling together in my tone. "You asked me here to talk, yet it sounds like you've already decided not to give our marriage a chance."

"I told you the other day at Dad's house that I wanted a divorce," she said, refusing to meet my eyes.

"Shit, Shel, we haven't discussed anything at all. You won't accept my calls. You won't see me. You're just jumping straight to ending it. I mean, have you thought of counseling or anything? I'll do whatever it takes, Shelly."

She shook her head sadly at me. "Cal, I don't think I'll ever be able to get over the fact that you slept with someone else, after six years of being together. I hate it. I can't even stand to think about it. You betrayed me."

The last she said in a whisper, making the full effect of her words wash over me like a million tiny pinpricks.

"I don't want a divorce," I responded, reaching for her hand. She took it quickly off of the table before I could touch her. "I love you, Shelly, and I'm willing to do anything."

"There's nothing you can do."

"I'll quit drinking. Never go out with the guys again. I'll prove to you how much I love and respect you, Shel."

"That's not a life, Cal. I don't want you to give up everything and never leave my sight. I want what we had, a relationship of love and trust, and I just don't think it's possible for me to have that relationship with you again."

I felt desperate, frantic at the thought of losing her.

"I won't sign divorce papers."

Shelly's head shot up and her green eyes bore into me.

"Why would you want to make this harder? I don't want to fight with you, Cal."

"I'm sorry, I don't want to make it harder, and I don't want to fight *with* you," I implored. "But I will fight *for* you, Shelly. Give me a chance to."

She was shaking her head again, and a plan

formulated in my mind.

"Give me eight weeks," I said desperately.

"I'm not going to live with you for eight weeks, Cal."

"No, I get that," I responded. "Give me eight Saturdays. Eight dates where it's just the two of us. Give me time to show you why we're so good together, and that I'm willing to bend and compromise to make our marriage work."

Shelly looked at me thoughtfully.

"Why eight?"

"One week for each year that we've been together."

"Eight weeks?" she asked, as if trying to decide whether she could stand to wait that long.

I nodded, hoping my outside looked calmer than my insides.

Shelly was quiet for a few minutes. I sat there, scared to death that she'd say no, but hopeful that she'd agree.

Finally, she looked me in the eye and started to talk.

"I want to move forward on selling the house. We need to move our stuff out and divvy everything up. I won't put everything on hold for eight weeks, but if it will take eight dates to get you to sign the paperwork, *without a fight*, I'll agree."

The thought of moving out, living separately, and selling our house made me fear that one day a week with her may not be enough to get Shelly to realize she still loved me, but desperate times called for desperate measures.

"Okay, I'll get my stuff out, and we can have Sasha put the house up for sale, but I want eight real dates, Shelly. You have to keep an open mind, and give me a chance."

"They will be just dates, Cal. No sex."

"We can play that by ear," I said. When she looked at me warily I added, "I'm not going to attack you, Shel. Give me a break."

"Sorry," she said softly. "I just want to establish rules. And, Cal, you need to know, I don't think eight weeks is going to change anything. I'm still going to want a divorce."

"Please," I pleaded desperately. "Give it a shot."

She nodded again, then stood to leave.

"I'll contact Sasha when I get home."

I sat there as she walked away, watched her drive off, then stared up at the old oak.

Shit, I had to come up with eight dates. They had to be romantic or mean something to us as a couple. Maybe I had to think of some things that she always wanted to do, but we hadn't done because of me, to show her that I was willing to do whatever she wanted in order to keep her as my wife.

I needed to get together with Scott and TJ and get some advice. They'd certainly been on a lot more dates than I had.

Chapter 10 - Shelly

I was feeling pretty good.

The rum and Cokes had gone down smoothly, and the pretty stud in my nose was only a little tender.

I laughed out loud as Gaby tried to fight off guys on the dance floor. With her long blonde hair braided down her back, and her skirt so long it grazed the floor as she moved, she looked like a free-spirited hippie. When Gaby moved, her body fluid and graceful, guys always paid attention.

"I'm gonna go save her," Sasha said with a wicked grin as she downed another shot of tequila.

I watched as Sasha sauntered over and crooked her finger at the guys Gaby was trying to dance away from. They went willingly, and Sasha was soon a blur of long legs and flashes of red as she danced seductively in between the two men.

I grinned at Gaby as she came toward me with

a scowl.

"Why do guys think that because I'm dancing, I want them to grind all over me?" Gaby asked, picking up her beer as she sat at the bar next to me. "I just want to enjoy the music."

"It's one of the hazards of looking hot and dancing in the middle of a club," I said, snickering when Gaby stuck her tongue out at me.

"It's good to hear you laugh," Gaby said, touching her hand to my shoulder.

I nodded. "It feels good too."

"So, you really sure about this eight weeks thing?"

I took a sip of my drink, shrugged, and said, "He said he'd sign the papers if I did it."

"What time are you guys meeting up tomorrow?"

"Cal said he'd pick me up around five."

"Did he say what you were going to do?"

"No, just said to dress casual when I asked."

"Hmmm," Gaby mumbled as she sipped her beer. "It's kind of cool though, huh? That he's going to plan surprise dates for eight weeks."

Gaby's blue eyes looked large and hopeful.

"Don't get your hopes up, Gabs," I said, putting my hand over hers. "Like I said, we're packing up the house on Sunday and it's going on the market. I fully intend to go through with the divorce when the eight weeks are up."

Gaby pouted a bit, but nodded at my words. "I'm here for you."

"I know," I said with a small smile. "Now let's stop talking about this depressing shit. How about a shot?"

"Okay," Gaby agreed as she waved the bartender over. He was yet another man who was hoping for a shot with her, so we never had a problem getting served whenever we came.

I ordered three, then turned to get Sasha's attention and waved her over.

All eyes watched as Sasha picked the hair up off of her neck to allow some cool air to sooth her. Her chest heaved from exertion, and the little red dress she wore left little to the imagination. Her face held a knowing smirk.

"You're such an attention whore," Gaby said when Sasha reached us.

"You know you love it," Sasha replied, blowing her a kiss.

Gabby laughed.

"I really do," she admitted.

"Here ya go," I said as I passed out the shots.

When we raised our glasses Gaby said, "To us ... To always having each other's backs, good times or bad. And to Sasha, whose sexy ass can distract the most annoying of men."

"Here, here," Sasha and I said in unison, grinning like fools.

We slammed the shot glasses on the table and I winced as the tequila burned its way down my throat.

"Shit," Gaby said suddenly.

I had barely looked up and followed her gaze when Sasha said, "I got this," and stormed off.

I looked to the front of the bar and the liquor turned harshly in my stomach when I saw Cal, Scott, and TJ walking in.

I kept my eyes on them as they all turned to watch Sasha approach. I was sure she shouted something at them, but couldn't hear from where I was sitting.

"Wanna get closer?" Gaby asked.

Sasha in full temper put on a great show.

I shook my head, my eyes locked on the scene before me.

Sasha strode up, hands on hips, and I could tell by the guys' faces that she was letting them have it. TJ broke away from the group and walked up to get toe to toe with Sasha. I could see the argument intensify. She was shaking her fist at him, and he leaned in to tower over her as he spoke back. Where

Sasha was loud and feisty when she was mad, TJ was soft and menacing. They made a magnificent sight.

Gaby and I had a bet in high school over how long it would take before the two of them hooked up. I'd guessed a week, and she'd guessed before graduation. We'd both been wrong. They couldn't see what everyone around them thought was obvious. They were a ticking time bomb.

I looked to the right and frowned when I saw Cal looking at me intently. I hurriedly turned my gaze back to the standoff.

Sasha was throwing her hands in the air, then she turned and stomped back over to us. I watched as the guys walked to the back of the bar, on the opposite side of where we were sitting.

"They're going to stay away from us, but they're staying," Sasha huffed when she got back.

I shrugged. "It's their favorite bar too. It's a small town, Sasha, I won't be able to avoid them."

I was sad that it felt like I had to. I hated to cause this riff between my friends.

"You know, you guys don't have to stop hanging out with them just because Cal and I are separated. They're still your friends too."

They both nodded, but I knew that the issues between Cal and I were bleeding over into our friendships, and I didn't know what I could do to stop it.

Chapter 11 - Cal

She looked so beautiful. It felt like forever since I'd been able to look at her. Just look at her. The guys were talking, but I wasn't paying attention to what they were saying. I was watching Shelly talk and laugh with Gaby and Sasha.

"Is that a nose ring?" I asked softly, not realizing that I was speaking out loud until TJ looked at me and asked, "Huh?"

I tore my gaze away from the girls and looked at my friends.

"It looks like Shelly got a nose ring. A little stud," I replied. "It looks good on her."

"Really?" Scott asked, turning in his seat and straining to see around a couple of big dudes that were in his line of sight.

"Stop being so obvious, man," TJ said, hitting Scott on the arm.

"What?" Scott asked with a scowl. "So, now, in

addition to apparently not being allowed in our favorite bar, we aren't allowed to look at the girls either?"

TJ shrugged and I said, "I'm sorry, guys." They both turned their focus on me, eyes wary. "I really messed things up."

"Hey, brother, you don't have to apologize to us," Scott said. "I just don't see why the girls are turning this into a group divorce."

"No one's getting a divorce," I said harshly as I stood up. I suddenly needed to get away from everyone and get some air.

"You aren't leaving, are ya?" TJ asked.

"Hey, I'm sorry," Scott said at the same time. "I didn't mean anything by it."

"I just need air," I said before I turned and walked back out the way we'd come in.

As soon as the air hit me in the face, I started to cool off and calm down a bit. The thought of Shelly actually going through with the divorce was unbearable to me. I couldn't stomach it. She was the only girl I'd ever loved, and I knew that as long as I lived, she was the only girl I'd ever want to spend my life with.

"Hey, Cal," a high-pitched voice said from my right.

I turned to see Melody Cannon barreling

toward me down the sidewalk. Melody had gone to school with us, and had always tried to weasel her way into our group. If I remembered correctly, I think TJ'd slept with her at some point, but it was hard to keep track.

"Oh, hey, Melody," I returned, trying to walk around her. She put her hand on my arm to stop me.

"I was sorry to hear about you and Shelly," she said, looking anything but sorry.

"Shelly and I are fine," I said tightly.

Melody's expression turned confused. "Oh ... I'd heard that you were getting a divorce."

"We are not getting a divorce," I said through gritted teeth. People were really starting to piss me off with this shit.

"But, I hear you're living separately and selling your house," she replied.

"We're fine, Melody. I'll see you around."

I was ready to go home. Forget the guys' night out.

I shook Melody's hand off of my arm and started toward my car.

"If you need comfort, or someone to talk to, give me a call, Cal," Melody called out behind me.

Jesus, I thought, but kept walking without dignifying that with a response.

I texted TJ and Scott and told them that I'd left.

Scott could give TJ a ride home, since he and I had rode together from work. I knew they'd understand. It was just too much to handle being in the same bar with Shelly and not being able to talk to her, let alone touch her.

I missed my wife.

I let myself into Scott's apartment, putting my keys and wallet on the table by the door. Scott liked everything to be in a certain place. His apartment was neater than any bachelor pad I'd ever seen, but Scott had always been that way.

He'd been raised by strict parents, who believed that kids should be seen and not heard, and had lived in a pretty sterile environment. There were no dinners or sleepovers at Scott's house growing up; we'd always gone to my house for that.

Compared to Scott's family, mine was like something out of the 1950s. My parents were still together, and my brother and I had been raised with a lot of freedom. Mine was usually the house that we all ended up hanging out at, and my parents liked it that way. They loved my friends, and they loved Shelly beyond belief.

I hadn't told them any of it. Not that I moved out, or why, or that Shelly wanted a divorce. I didn't have the heart to break theirs, and I was also horribly ashamed to tell them about Vegas. I knew how disappointed they would be in me. Especially my mom. I knew I'd have to tell them eventually, but I just wasn't ready yet. It was hard enough letting Shelly down, I couldn't handle my family's reaction.

I sat down on the couch that had become my bed, and picked up the remote. I turned it to ESPN and settled back, not really paying attention. I looked around Scott's place, and felt the sudden urge to mess something up. I chuckled when I thought of Scott's reaction. He'd probably kick me out.

When my gaze landed on a picture of Scott and his fiancée, my face fell.

Victoria.

Just her name sounded snooty.

I hated the fact that Scott was marrying someone exactly like his mother, because I knew she'd make him miserable, but he was convinced that he was in love.

TJ and I had both tried to talk to him about Victoria, to try and understand what he loved about her, and why he wanted to spend the rest of his life with her, but Scott had started to get upset and defensive, so we let it go. She wasn't worth losing our friend over, but I couldn't help but hope that Scott realized his mistake before it was too late.

I sprawled out on the couch facing the ceiling and my thoughts went to my date with Shelly tomorrow. I wanted to do something that she loved to do, but I didn't, so I came up with karaoke for the first date. She and the girls went and sang karaoke quite a bit, but the guys and I never went along. I couldn't carry a tune to save my life, and I hated being up in front of large groups of people.

I hoped that things would go well and we would be able to have a nice time together. I wanted so much for things to go back to the way they used to be, but I knew we had a long road ahead of us. I just hoped that this was a step in the right direction.

Chapter 12 – Shelly

I fluffed out my hair and stared at myself in the mirror, amazed to realize that I was nervous about being alone with Cal.

I'd never been nervous around him, other than the initial butterflies when we started dating in high school; normally, Cal made me feel comfortable and at ease.

Maybe I was more worried about dealing with the pain that I felt whenever I looked at him now. His betrayal hurt, as much now as it had a few weeks ago, and I wasn't sure how I could stand to go on a date with him, knowing what he did to our marriage.

I knew that I couldn't forgive him. Not yet. But would I be able to go through with these dates? Not only did I not want to be put in uncomfortable situations, but I didn't want to give Cal false hope. I also didn't want to hurt him more than I knew I already was. Yes, he'd hurt me, but I loved him enough to not want to see him in pain.

It was an all-around fucked-up situation.

I gave myself one more glance when the doorbell rang, and shrugged. He'd said casual, so jeans and a T-shirt would have to work.

"Hey," I said to Cal when I opened the door.

He looked so handsome in the dark blue polo shirt I'd gotten him for his birthday that I had to momentarily shut my eyes and take a deep breath, to try and ease the constant ache that had taken up residence in my heart. His dark hair was mussed, and he had a five o'clock shadow. I loved it when he looked scruffy.

"You okay?" Cal asked.

My eyes fluttered open and I let out the breath.

"I'll be fine," I looked up into his dark eyes and said. "But I'd like to follow you, rather than drive together."

Cal's shoulders sagged a bit, but he nodded his acceptance of my request. I picked my purse up off the hook by the door, and closed the door behind me.

I got into my truck and turned up the radio when I heard Hunter Hayes singing about love.

I followed Cal's Mustang along the familiar streets, and looked up in surprise when he pulled in to the karaoke bar that Gaby, Sasha, and I liked to frequent.

No way was Cal going to sing karaoke, I thought with a giggle. The man could not carry a tune.

When I saw him get out of his car, the smile left my face as visions of him with another woman slammed into my head.

My eyes filled and I dropped my gaze, telling myself quietly to pull it together.

I just had to get through these next eight weeks.

"You okay?" Cal asked again as he opened the door for me.

I looked up at him, not bothering to try and mask the pain that I was sure showed on my face.

He'd put it there, so he deserved to see it.

"I will be," I said again. I thought about adding, "*In eight weeks.*" But that seemed like an unnecessarily cruel thing to say, so I bit my tongue.

I could tell by the frown on his face that Cal had gotten my meaning.

"Cal," I began, placing my hand gently on his arm. "This isn't a good idea. We're just going to keep hurting each other."

"Shelly, it'll be fine. Please just give it a shot," Cal pleaded.

I dropped my hand and nodded. I locked my truck and led the way inside.

It was kind of early, but I walked straight to the bar and ordered a gin and tonic.

Cal walked up next to me and asked for a beer, then turned to me with a small smile and said, "I really like your piercing."

My hand flew up to the little stud in my nose, and I smiled at the fact that I'd actually gotten it. I was surprised at Cal's reaction though.

"You do?"

"Yeah, it looks really good on you."

I stared at him, confused, then smiled when he turned toward the sounds coming from the stage. His face morphed into one of horror, his beer halfway to his lips.

I laughed, then turned and walked toward a table in the middle of the room and sat down.

I'd seen the girl who was on stage perform many times … She never seemed to get any better, but what she lacked in talent, she made up for in enthusiasm.

The chair screeched a bit when Cal went to sit down, and he looked around the room with an expression of apology. He looked totally nervous and out of his element.

"So," I turned to him and asked. "What next?"

"We're going to sing," Cal said softly, his eyes wide with fear.

"*We*?" I couldn't help but mess with him.

Cal nodded as he drank his beer as if it was water, and he'd just spent days in the desert.

"You first," I challenged.

He'd said he was going to prove to me that he was willing to do anything to make our marriage work, and although I didn't think it was possible, I was willing to watch him suffer.

Cal finished his beer, then pushed slowly away from the table, his chair scraping with every inch.

He walked over to the DJ like a man on death row, and I couldn't help the glee that coursed through me.

This was going to be fun.

I sipped my gin and tonic and watched Cal shaking his head as the DJ rattled off possible songs. Finally, he nodded and made his way to the stage.

He looked visibly shaken, and I started to regret the thrill I'd felt over his nervousness. He looked like he was about to vomit all over the stage. Cal gripped the microphone so hard that his knuckles were white. He stared at the monitor, probably wishing that his three minutes of fame were behind him.

When the music started to play, I let out a loud laugh, causing Cal to look up and catch my eye. The smile that spread over his face turned my insides to mush.

As he sang *All Summer Long*, by Kid Rock, memories of our summer before senior year flashed through my mind.

We'd been dating for six months and were so in love. Our summer was spent at the lake with Sasha, Gaby, TJ, and Scott. We went out on the boat, played in the water, and stayed up late at bonfires.

It was the best summer of my life.

We were young, carefree, and with the people we loved most in the world. It had seemed like the world was ours for the taking, and we'd hoped the summer would never end.

When the song ended, Cal's ears were bright red and he left the stage like his jeans were on fire.

When he plopped into the chair next to me, I turned to him, the memory of the song still a smile on my lips.

"That wasn't so bad, was it?"

Cal looked to me, his face totally serious, and said, "That was the most terrifying experience of my life."

We shared a laugh, and he gestured toward the stage with his head.

"Your turn."

I gave him a smile and a nod, then went over to the familiar DJ and gave him thumbs up.

I sang the same song every time I came here.

I grew up loving to sing, but had never sung in public until Sasha and Gaby had brought me here on a girls' night. Once we'd made it a regular hangout, I'd grown to love the feel of being on stage with the mic in my hand. I knew it would never be anything other than a hobby, but singing made me feel a peace, in a way not many other things in my life ever had.

I let myself feel the music as the words that Adele had written sprang from my lips. I closed my eyes and sang from my heart. It was the most content I'd felt in weeks.

When the music stopped, I opened my eyes to the sound of applause and was surprised to see Cal on his feet, a look of awe on his face.

I smiled shyly and walked off of the stage.

Before I knew what was happening, I was swept up in Cal's arms as he spun me in a circle.

"That was amazing, Shel," Cal said, his voice filled with excitement.

When my feet hit the floor I gently maneuvered myself out of his arms. My heart was pounding, and confusion filled me.

I took a step back and said, "Thanks."

Cal hadn't yet realized the distance I was trying to put between us; he was still gushing about my performance.

"I can't believe I didn't know what a beautiful voice you have. I mean, you always sound good in the shower and when we're driving, but I had no idea just how powerful it was until now." Cal's eyes were lit up with excitement and his grin was contagious.

Although I didn't want him to put his arms around me again, I did feel pride at his words.

To try and keep the situation from getting awkward, I said, "Okay, now let's do one together."

The excitement fell from his face and I laughed at the look that replaced it.

"You'll be fine," I said with a chuckle. "Don't be a baby."

Determination settled on Cal's face. He was never one to back down from a challenge.

"Okay," he said, taking my hand and leading me back to the stage.

Luckily, it was early enough that the only people in the audience were regulars, so we didn't have to wait in line or fight for a turn to sing. I couldn't imagine the terror that Cal would have felt if we had a packed house.

Rather than jerk my hand out of his, I allowed it, but I was very conscious of the feelings holding his hand evoked: trepidation, longing, and contentment.

I needed to focus and remember why we were even on this "date."

"Any duet is fine," Cal said to the DJ as we walked passed him and up the steps.

I grabbed the mic and watched as someone walked over and gave Cal another one. We looked at each other, then turned to the screen.

My mind was filled with so many warnings and contradictions that I didn't even pay attention to the music, but just started singing when the words popped on the screen.

I looked over at Cal and when he sang, *"I can't look at you, when I'm lying next to her,"* the words penetrated and I dropped the mic.

I flew off the stage, down the stairs, and out the door, tears streaming down my face.

"Shelly, wait," Cal called out from behind me.

I stopped and turned, not bothering to wipe the tears or hide the fact that with one sentence the scab that had been forming over my heart was ripped off.

"I'm sorry," Cal said helplessly. He ran his hands through his hair and looked around the parking lot before turning back to face me, with sorrow in his eyes. "I didn't know what song they were gonna play."

"I know," I said sadly. "This is just too hard."

"No, Shelly, please." Cal stepped toward me, but stopped himself from touching me. "Please, don't give up. Give us these eight weeks."

I brought my eyes to his and nodded slightly. "I have to go."

Cal didn't say anything, just watched me leave. He was still standing there when I looked back in my rearview mirror.

Chapter 13 - Cal

This day sucked.

After screwing up my first date with Shelly, I'd gone home and had a few beers with Scott, driving him crazy by whining about how I needed to win Shelly back. Then, this morning, I'm faced with the fact that my friends and I are all getting together to pack up my house, so that Shelly and I can separate our belongings and sell the house we'd loved so much.

I swear, she and I must have looked at twenty-five houses before we'd agreed on the little fixer-upper five miles from where we'd grown up. The fact that we were really going through with selling it broke my heart.

I was worried that without tangible proof of our marriage together, it would be easier for Shelly to walk away.

I hoped I was wrong.

It was hard to hold on to that hope, though, when the same four people who had helped us move into this house were helping us move out.

"TJ, I swear to God, if you don't give me back that packing tape this instant, I'm going to kick you right in your flat ass!" I heard Sasha yell from the other room.

"Red, you know my ass is perfect," TJ yelled back. "That's why you haven't been able to take your eyes off of it for the past six years."

"You wish, you egomaniac. The only way I'd stare at your ass, is if you had a picture of Henry Cavill stapled to it."

I chuckled at the familiar banter of two of my closest friends. I'd missed this over the past few weeks. And even though we were all together under the worst possible circumstance, I was happy that we were all together again.

I tried to pack quickly, without paying too much attention to what I was doing. I was afraid if I didn't, I'd break down and embarrass myself, and I'd already done enough of that. I walked into the kitchen and paused when I saw Scott and Gaby standing by the sink, his hand on her arm, and their heads bent together in deep discussion.

I assumed they were just having a conversation, but when I said, "What's up?" and they jumped apart guiltily and looked up at me with surprise, I wondered what was going on.

"Nothing," they said simultaneously.

I tilted my head and looked at them, searching their faces for a clue as to what they could possibly have to look guilty about. Figuring they were talking about Shelly and me, I shrugged and said, "Okay." Then I walked to the fridge to grab a water and get back to work.

When I walked past the living room, I saw Shelly sitting on the floor going through our CDs. She was holding a Brad Paisley CD in one hand, and wiping a tear off of her face with the other. It was the CD that featured out wedding song.

My chest tight, I walked into the room and crouched down onto the floor next to her.

"Remember the first time we heard that CD?" I asked softly.

Shelly looked up at me, her eyes big and sad. She nodded, but I answered anyway, caught up in the past.

"I snuck in to your house after the Sadie Hawkins dance, and you picked it out of your dad's collection. We danced to the entire thing, even the songs that were impossible to dance to." I chuckled as I remembered that night. "We laughed so loud, your dad came down and caught us. I thought he was going to kick me out, but he didn't, he just told me that if I got fresh, he'd grab his rifle."

I looked into Shelly's eyes, and we both smiled at the memory.

"When they asked what song I wanted to dance to at our wedding, there was no doubt in my mind what song to pick," Shelly added softly, her voice rough with tears.

I squatted there next to her for a moment longer, visions of that night dancing through my head.

We looked at each other, neither of us speaking, and I knew we were both reflecting on what we were about to lose.

As much as I wanted to deny even the remote possibility that my relationship with Shelly would end, I knew that we couldn't go on the way that we were now.

I yearned for the couple that we used to be.

When the pain became too much to bear, I stood and said, "Well, I'd better get back to it." Then I turned and went back to finish packing up the bathroom with a heavy heart.

As I listened to the sounds of our friends whispering in the other room, I packed and labeled boxes for Shelly and myself.

My stomach burned as I divided all of our

stuff, most of which we had bought together. It wasn't hard to figure out who got what; I packed most of it for Shelly. All I needed were the bare essentials. Plus, I was holding out hope that in eight weeks, we'd be moving back in together and moving forward with the rest of our life.

My mind kept returning to the night before, and I knew I had to come up with a date that didn't have the potential to backfire like last night's date had. Convincing Shelly that I loved her implicitly, that she could trust me, and that we belonged together, was my only focus at this point.

There was no future for me without Shelly in it. I just needed to convince her of the same.

Chapter 14 - Shelly

Was this ever going to get easier?

I cried myself to sleep again last night. After packing up our home on Sunday, the girls and I went back and cleaned the house on Monday, to get it ready for Sasha to show it. I didn't tell Cal, or ask the guys to come help, because after Sunday, I didn't think I could stand the pain that came from all of us being together.

I hated how awkward it was, and I wished there was something I could do to change it.

After we were done cleaning, I'd taken my time and walked around the house. I ran my hand along the countertops, remembering the first dinner I'd cooked for Cal. Meatloaf, with mashed potatoes, gravy, and corn on the cob.

Cal loved my meatloaf.

I smiled when I looked over the stencils I'd painted in the bathroom. They were delicate white flowers against the baby blue walls. Cal had joked that he'd wanted the bathroom to be done in a fishing theme, but I'd bought the stencils and had the bathroom decorated by the time he'd gotten home from work. He'd pretended to be angry, but I said I'd make up for it, and we'd ended up having sex right there. He'd lifted me up against the wall, and when my legs wrapped around his waist, the decor of the bathroom was quickly forgotten.

I couldn't walk into any room of our home without a memory of Cal and me making love coming through. We'd always had a wonderful sex life, and I'd often had a hard time keeping my hands off of him. Cal was one of the sexiest and most handsome men I'd ever seen. And he was all mine.

At least … he had been.

Now, I was sitting at my desk at the bank, trying not to think about Sasha showing my house to prospective buyers. I should be ecstatic that she already had people interested in seeing the house, but my heart hurt when I thought of someone living in the home Cal and I had built together.

It had been my decision to sell it, but I hadn't realized how hard it would be.

I sighed deeply and pushed back from my desk.

I needed coffee.

I walked into the break room, started fixing a cup, and turned when I heard the door open behind me.

"Oh, hey, Carlos," I said when the small loans officer walked in.

"Hi, Shelly, how are you today?" Carlos asked with a smile.

Carlos had been working with me at the bank for about three months. He was new to the area and was really sweet. He was good-looking and kind, a single dad of a little boy.

"Okay," I lied with a smile. "How about you?"

Carlos walked over and filled his cup. He looked down for a minute, just standing there with his steaming mug in his hand, then he cleared his throat and looked up at me sheepishly.

"Look, Shelly," he began. "I don't want to step out of line, but I heard that you're separated from your husband, and that you're getting a divorce."

My stomach dropped at his words. It felt weird hearing that sentence spoken aloud.

I tucked my hair behind my ear, my hands shaking. "Um, yeah. We are separated."

Carlos looked nervous and took a deep breath before saying, "I know it's probably too soon, but I'd love to take you out, once you're ready."

My eyes widened. I was afraid they might bug

out of my head, but I tried to remain calm otherwise.

Shit, I didn't know what to do. Everyone had always known about me and Cal, so I'd never had to worry about guys asking me out.

"Wow," I managed to spit out. "Um, I don't know what to say ... Cal and I are separated, but we have this deal where I won't ask for a divorce for eight weeks, while we try to make our marriage work." I spoke so quickly, I hoped Carlos was able to make out what I was saying. I liked him, and I didn't want to hurt his feelings, but I was in no way ready to even think about dating someone else. At least not while I was dating my husband. "I appreciate the offer though."

Carlos looked embarrassed, and my heart went out to him. I'm sure it took a lot of courage to ask someone out, and I hoped this wouldn't make things awkward between us.

He nodded and said softly, "That's great. Please, forget I said anything. But, if you need to talk ... I've been there."

I smiled and nodded my consent. When he walked out, I sagged against the counter. I wasn't sure how much more emotional upheaval I was going to be able to take.

I pulled out my cell phone and sent a text to Sasha and Gaby, "*Carlos from work just asked me out.*"

I knew that Gaby was probably too busy at work to check her phone, but Sasha always had hers in her hand, so I wasn't surprised when my phone beeped almost immediately.

"Of course he did, we are so going to rule this city."

I chuckled at her response. I knew Sasha was trying to make me feel better. She loved Cal and although she'd never say it for fear of feeling unsupportive, she was hoping that we'd be able to work it out. I appreciated the gesture though.

"I said no."

"No fear, he was the first of many. Lunch?"

I smiled and said that I'd love to meet for lunch. Now I had to figure out how to get through the next few hours.

Chapter 15 - Cal

The last few days I'd fallen into a routine. Get up, go to work, have dinner with TJ, go back to Scott's, have a beer with him (if he's not out with Victoria), then go to bed and repeat.

It wasn't exciting, but at least I wasn't still moping on Scott's couch.

Last week's date hadn't gone the way I'd planned, and packing up our house had been painful, but I wasn't giving up hope.

Today I'd asked Shelly to be ready, and hungry, at eleven. I stood at Shelly's dad's door and took a deep breath before knocking.

Shelly opened the door with a timid smile on her face, that didn't quite reach her eyes. I'm sure she was thinking back to the pain we'd both experienced last weekend, and I really hoped that today we could just enjoy each other's company.

"Hey," she said softly as she walked outside.

She was dressed in jeans and a bright green top. I loved it when Shelly wore green, it made her eyes pop and made it seem like she was lit up from the inside out.

Her hair was shorter. It still fell past her shoulders in waves, but now it had some sort of highlights running through it.

"You look beautiful," I said honestly.

Shelly blushed lightly, then put a hand to her hair. "Thanks."

"Are you ready to go?"

"Sure," she said, bringing her eyes up to mine. "I'll follow you."

My stomach clenched a bit, but I nodded. I didn't know if she wanted to ride separately because she didn't want to have small talk in the car, or if she wanted a quick getaway. I got it, either way, but I hoped she'd eventually feel comfortable enough to ride with me.

The drive to the park didn't take long. Bellows Park was vast and green, with playgrounds, a dog park, a pond, and plenty of space to enjoy a meal.

I got out and met Shelly at her door. I opened it for her and held out my hand to help her out.

She took it and rose out of the car, then paused and looked at me.

"Bellows Park," she stated softly.

This was where I'd brought her on our first date. I was hoping to recreate that day, and the feelings that went with it, and I could tell by the look on her face, she knew it.

I walked around her car to mine, and opened my trunk. I pulled out a blanket and a picnic basket, then turned and smiled at Shelly.

"You ready?"

She nodded and I started off toward the spot by the pond that we'd picnic'd at all those years ago.

The weather had been perfect that day, and Shelly had looked amazingly beautiful in a pair of black shorts and a black-and-white striped top. Her hair had been pulled back into ponytail, and her face was fresh and pretty.

We'd come to the park with a lunch packed by my mother, but I never told Shelly that; I'd claimed that I'd made it all myself. I wanted to impress her, but I knew she saw right through me. She always did.

We'd spent the afternoon feeding ducks and nibbling on the food in the basket, as we told each other all of our hopes and dreams. We'd even rented a paddleboat and took it out to the middle of the pond. It was out there, in the center of the pond, with the sun setting, that I'd gathered the courage to lean in to her, and initiated our first kiss.

When we reached the edge of the pond, I laid out the blanket and placed the basket on the edge.

"Do you want to sit and eat, or do you want to feed the ducks first?" I asked Shelly when she looked to me for guidance.

She smiled slowly. "Ducks."

I opened the basket, pulled out half a loaf of bread, and handed it to her. The look on her face was childlike, and it warmed my heart. I hadn't seen her look so unburdened since our anniversary.

We walked over to the ducks, and I watched her as she opened the bag and tore off pieces of bread. She leaned over at the waist to throw some out to the ducks, and I took the opportunity to allow my gaze to travel her body. My own body began to harden as I watched Shelly's jeans strain against her backside.

Shit, I needed to calm myself down before I ended up upsetting her. I didn't want anything to ruin this date. Even my own desires for my wife.

Baseball, grandma, possums, cookies ...

By the time Shelly turned to me, a big grin on her face, I'd managed to get my hormones in check.

"I haven't been out here in forever, it looks great," Shelly said, her gaze sweeping the pond and its surrounding areas. "Do they still have paddleboats?"

I wondered if she was thinking back to our first kiss, and said, "Yeah, they sure do. I thought we'd rent one after we eat."

She offered me a piece of bread, and I took it gently from her hand before throwing it out to the waiting ducks. A couple of them went after it, and Shelly laughed when they started quacking at each other.

"How's everything at work?" I asked as she threw the last piece of bread.

"It's been okay," she said quietly. "I haven't been very focused, I'll admit, but everyone's been understanding."

Her answer made me wish I'd brought up something else. I needed to think of safe topics. Things that would make her happy, not sad.

As we walked back to the blanket, she asked, "How about you? Work okay?"

I held out my hand to help her down on the blanket, and she took it with a small smile. I felt the warmth of her hand in mine, and wished that I could pull her to me, but I knew it was too soon.

I feared I'd never get to hold her in my arms again, but I shook it off and forced myself to remain positive. If I didn't believe Shelly could forgive me, why would she?

After she was seated, I followed suit and sat

with my legs stretched out in front of me.

"It's been good, kind of slow, but TJ's been keeping me entertained."

"I bet."

"He told me this story the other day about a girl he picked up in Walmart. He walked right up to her, handed her his phone, and told her to program her number in, so he could call before he came over to pick her up at eight."

"Did she give it to him?" Shelly asked with a smile. She loved TJ stories.

"She sure did, didn't even bat an eye. Once he had her number, TJ walked away giving her a wink and a smile."

The sound of Shelly's laughter warmed me up from the inside out. There's nothing I wouldn't do to hear that sound for the rest of my life.

As we ate, we kept to the safe topics, talking about our friends and family. It was a wonderful meal, and when we were done eating Shelly asked playfully, "So, did your mother pack this basket for you?"

"Nope," I responded with a grin. "I made it all myself."

We both knew I was lying, I had no game when it came to cooking. I'd picked everything up, ready to eat, at the supermarket. I was thrilled that

Shelly was joking with me, just like she used to.

I stood up and held out my hand to her.

"The paddleboats await." She put her hand in mine and I helped her to her feet. When we started in the direction of the rentals, I kept holding her hand, hopeful that she wouldn't pull away.

She didn't.

When we got to the rental booth, I reluctantly let her hand go so I could pay for the boat.

"I haven't been in a paddleboat since the last time we were here," I said as I guided her to the blue boat we had rented.

"Me neither," Shelly responded. "I don't know why not, I remember we had fun."

"I guess we just got caught up in life," I admitted. "We didn't take enough days off to do something fun."

Once we were both seated, we started paddling toward the middle of the water.

"This hurts more then I remember," I said with a laugh.

"We aren't sixteen anymore," Shelly replied.

Once we got well off shore, we stopped paddling and let the boat float along in the water.

"Doesn't that sound peaceful?" Shelly asked, and I tuned in to the sounds of the water lapping against the boat, the birds chirping, and a dog barking off in the distance.

"Yeah, it does."

I turned to look at her profile, and smiled when the stud in her nose blinked in the sunlight. She looked at peace sitting there with her face upturned and eyes half closed, basking in the sun.

She opened her eyes and turned her to face me, that small smile still on her lips, and without thinking, I leaned in. I barely registered the widening of her eyes before my lips caressed hers softly.

Her lips were soft and full, and although I wanted to deepen the kiss, instead I pulled back and smiled at her.

Shelly didn't look angry or yell, she just sat very still and looked into my eyes. We sat there for a moment, neither of us speaking, just feeling. I knew that my body was a mix of emotions from that kiss, and I'd wager that she felt the same way.

We paddled back, and although I wanted to go home with her and spend the night cradling her in my arms, I knew it was time for this date to come to an end.

When I walked her to her car I said, "Thanks for coming with me today, Shelly."

"You're welcome. It was fun."

I helped her into her car, and she gave me one more slightly confused look before she pulled out of the parking lot and left me there.

As I watched her leave me this time, rather than feeling the dread I had when she'd left me last weekend, I felt full of hope.

Chapter 16 - Shelly

I'd lain awake last night, reliving the events of yesterday's date in my head.

I'd felt happy, sad, and confused.

The day with Cal had been almost perfect. It had felt normal and familiar. We'd been *Us*.

Being with Cal that way, talking, laughing, and having fun, had made it easy to forget the pain of the last few weeks. And when he'd kissed me ... I'd wanted to sink into that feeling and pull him in closer.

I missed him.

I missed us.

I missed sex.

Seriously ... I missed the joy and comfort that came along with giving yourself fully to the person that you love. The utter abandon that came with having sex with that person. The contentment you felt afterwards, when you fell asleep in their arms.

That's how I'd always felt with Cal, and I missed sharing that with him.

I was beyond confused.

On one hand, I missed and loved my husband. On the other, I hated the way he'd betrayed me and made me feel.

I felt as if I were at war with myself. Now, I was preparing to move into a one-bedroom condo that Sasha had found for me. The current owners were looking for someone to rent to own, and I was about to become that person.

I was nervous and excited about living on my own. I'd gone straight from my dad's to being married and living with Cal, so I'd never lived alone.

I heard a knock and my dad talking, so I went out, expecting to see the girls, and was surprised to see Scott and TJ sitting on the sofa in the living room.

"Hey, guys," I said. "What's going on?"

Scott stood when he heard my voice and responded, "Gaby told me that you were moving today, so TJ and I thought we'd come help. We didn't want you ladies having fun without us."

TJ grinned and I smiled back at the two of them, then my smile dropped when I wondered if that meant Cal was coming too.

At the look on my face, Scott shook his head and said, "It's just us."

I briefly wondered what Cal was up to, but understood that him helping me move into a new place would be hard on both of us. Moving out of our house had been difficult enough.

"Thanks, guys."

"We're your friends too, Shel, no matter what happens," Scott responded with a sad smile.

I nodded and started to respond, when the door flew open and Sasha came whirling in.

She even made workout clothes look fabulous.

"Hey, Papa," she said, leaning in to give my dad a kiss on the cheek before turning to the rest of us. "Hey, guys. Let's get this party started."

We headed outside, where I already had the truck backed up in the driveway. All of my stuff was still in boxes in the garage, where we'd left it last week.

Gaby arrived in the mist of our loading up the truck, and jumped in to help out.

With six of us working, we had everything loaded up in no time, and were heading off to my new home. It wasn't much, but I was ready to be out of my father's house and back out on my own.

We made quick work of unloading the truck and I ordered pizza for everyone to thank them for helping me out. We were sitting around my new living room floor eating when Scott said, "I have to go, Victoria and I are meeting to plan our rehearsal dinner."

I noticed his eyes go straight to Gaby's. They looked at each other, seeming to have a private conversation with one look, before she turned her head and looked down at her pizza.

That was weird ...

"Okay," I responded. "Thanks again for coming and helping out. It would have taken us a lot longer without your muscles."

TJ stood, flexed dramatically, and said, "That's what all the ladies say."

Sasha snorted at that, and TJ leaned over and tweaked her nose.

"You love it," he said with a grin.

"Thanks again," I said with a chuckle, giving first TJ, then Scott, a hug.

I walked them to the door, and after TJ walked out I stopped Scott by placing my hand on his arm.

"Is he doing okay, Scott?" I asked quietly.

Scott looked at me, his deep brown eyes reflecting concern. "He misses you, Shel. Look, I know it's none of my business, but I've known Cal forever, and I know what you mean to him. He's a great guy, the best. He made a terrible mistake, and I feel horrible that this all came about at my bachelor party. We never should have let him leave. We never should have separated. I love you both and I hate to see you both in so much pain." He put his hands on my shoulders. "You have to know, Shel, he's gutted over this. No one will love you the way that he does. He will love you forever. Just think about that before you make any final decisions."

I nodded slowly, unable to stop tears from falling at his words. He lifted a hand and wiped them off of my cheek before pulling me in for another hug.

"You'll both get through this. I love ya, Shel."

He released me and walked out to where TJ was waiting, a look of sorrow on his face. I closed the door slowly, then turned and leaned against it, my eyes closed.

I heard feet approaching and opened my eyes to see Gaby coming toward me, a glass of wine in her hand.

"What do you say we have a drink, then get started on making this house a home?"

"Okay," I said, then laughed when Sasha ran over and pulled me into a bear hug.

It was great having friends who could see you through anything.

Chapter 17 - Cal

While the guys were over helping Shelly move into her new condo, I was pacing a hole in Scott's floor, telling myself over and over why I couldn't join them.

Oh, but I wanted to.

Even though it would hurt to see her moving in to a place without me, I would rather be with her and in pain, than without her and pain free.

I missed being with her.

I missed talking to her.

I missed lying with her in my arms.

I missed sex.

God, did I miss sex.

I didn't have anything to compare it to, because I still didn't remember sleeping with that blonde in Vegas, but sex with Shelly had been perfect. Just listening to Scott and TJ talk about their different sexual experiences, I knew that what Shelly and I had together was rare.

When I heard the key in the door, I froze and got ready to shoot a barrage of questions at Scott about Shelly's new place, but it was Victoria who walked through the door.

She entered and paused when she saw me in the living room. She didn't even bother to hide her distain.

Five foot seven, thin as a rail, and always dressed to impress, Victoria should have been impressive herself, with her sleek bob and perfectly manicured nails. The problem was, she was a total bitch, and that made her a troll in my eyes. I hated that she'd spun her web around Scott, and he seemed unable to see her for what she really was.

"Cal," Victoria said dryly. "Still imposing on Scott, I see."

"Victoria," I responded with a glare. "Scott's not here. Is there something that I can help you with? A new broom perhaps?"

She curled her lip and replied, "You always think you're so cool, don't you. Although ... it's not too cool to be sleeping on your old friend's couch, rather than in bed with your wife."

I saw red and was about to let her have it, when Scott walked in the still open door.

"Victoria!" he said softly, his tone dangerous. I

knew from the look on his face that he'd heard our exchange. "That's uncalled for. I wish the two of you would make an effort to get along ... For my sake."

I lowered my eyes, then looked back up and met Scott's gaze. He was right. He was my best friend, and I owed it to him to make more of an effort. As much as I loathed Victoria, she was a major part of his life, and if I didn't get on board, there was the possibility that I would lose him in mine.

I couldn't bear the thought of losing anyone else right now. Especially someone as important to me as Scott. He was like my brother.

"You're right, man. I apologize to you, and to Victoria. Let me get out of your hair for a while, so you guys can have some privacy."

"You don't have to leave, Cal," Scott replied.

"No worries," I said with a smile to both of them. Victoria didn't smile back or reply. Whatever, one of us had to be the bigger person. "I need to go see my folks anyway."

I walked out, leaving them to their evening of planning, and wondering how Scott was ever going to be happy with a woman like Victoria. I didn't understand why he put up with her. He knew what kind of person she was, it's not like she hid it.

I thought about Scott and Victoria's relationship on the drive to my parents, and came to the conclusion that I would never get it. I just needed to be there for my friends and try not to push my opinions on him. He was always there for me, no matter how horrible my mistakes, and I would do the same for him.

When I pulled up to my childhood home my stomach clenched as I thought of my parents, and the disappointment I knew would be apparent on their faces when they found out about me and Shelly.

I walked through the gate and up the stone path. I smiled at the pots of flowers covering the porch. My mother loved flowers, and she thrived on filling her home with them.

I took a deep breath and put my hand on the doorknob, then let it out as I opened the door and crossed the threshold.

I inhaled spicy cinnamon and tart apples, my mother's favorite scent. She was always known to have some potpourri, candles, and oils scattered throughout the house. This was the smell of my childhood.

"Hey, Cal, what's going on?" My brother was descending the stairs. I looked up and felt a surge of pride. Craig was a senior in high school and about to turn eighteen. He was smart, handsome, and a hell of a baseball player. He was my polar opposite, and I loved him for it.

"Not much, Craig, how's school?"

Craig walked over and put his arms around me briefly, before pulling away with a grin. We could have been twins. We were the exact same height, shared the same dark hair and facial features, but while I had dark brown eyes, his were an unnatural sea green. I'd never seen anything like it.

"Great, only a few months left, and the season is about to start," Craig answered. "I'll send you the schedule."

"Sounds good." I looked around the cozy living room and asked, "Mom around?"

"Yeah," Craig said, thrusting his head toward the back of the house. "I think she's in the kitchen making bread. Dad's out at the golf course."

I clapped my hand on his shoulder and said, "I'll come find you in a bit."

"Sorry, brother," he said, his grin cocky. "I've got a date."

"Shit." I grinned back. "Who allowed that?"

He just snorted at me, grabbed his jacket from the closet, and walked out with a wave.

I shook my head, then walked down the hallway toward the kitchen.

"Is that my long-lost son I hear?" My mother's amused voice reached me before I turned in to see her smiling face. She was standing at the island in the middle of the kitchen, her hands full of flour and dough as she kneaded.

"Hi, Mom," I walked over and kissed her on the top of her head. "Sorry I haven't been by recently."

She looked up at me with eyes that matched my own and said, "I figured your absence had something to do with the For Sale sign in front of your house."

I should have known better than to think I would be able to hide anything from my mother.

Chapter 18 - Shelly

I looked over and studied Cal's face as he drove. He looked deep in thought, with a small frown on his face. I wondered if I should ask him what was wrong, or stay out of it. I'd left him, after all, so I didn't think I had a right to pry. I hated to see Cal upset though; he was always such a positive person. If he was troubled, there was a good reason for it.

When he'd come by for our date, I'd met him outside, rather than having him come in the condo. I don't know if I was protecting him from the pain of seeing me on my own, or if I was protecting my newfound freedom. To ease the sting, I'd agreed to ride with him this time, rather than drive myself.

Now that we were in the car and on our way to date number three, I found myself struggling. Should I remain quiet, or ask him what was wrong.

Knowing Cal, he wouldn't feel better until he

got whatever was bothering him off his chest, so I asked, "Is everything okay?"

Cal turned briefly to look at me, almost as if he'd forgotten I was there, then turned his eyes back to the road before him.

He was quiet for a minute, which made me rethink my decision to pry, then he sighed deeply.

Uh-oh, a big sigh usually meant it was something personal, not work related.

If it was something personal, it probably had to do with our situation.

Maybe I didn't want to know ...

"I went by my parents' the other day," Cal began. "I had kind of been avoiding them since everything happened between us."

"Cal," I said, my voice filled with surprise. He told his parents everything. "You didn't tell them we were ... separated?"

"I couldn't, Shel," he responded. "Not only because I hope it's only temporary and I didn't want to worry them, but because I didn't want to disappoint them."

My heart thumped loudly in my chest.

"Cal, your parents adore you, you could never disappoint them."

He turned to me, his eyes filled with sorrow.

"They didn't raise their sons to cheat."

I felt my anger at this entire situation ease a bit in my gut. I loved Cal's folks, and they loved me, but more than anything, they loved their boys. I knew that it would be hard for him to admit to them that he wasn't perfect, and it would be hard for them to hear, but I had to believe that they loved him unconditionally.

We pulled off and into a parking lot. Cal turned off the car, but we both just sat there.

"Babe," I said, the endearment I'd always used for him rusty on my tongue. I reached out and touched his cheek. "They'll forgive you."

Cal's eyes bore into mine.

"Will you?"

I dropped my hand and answered honestly, "I don't know."

Cal nodded, and after a moment's pause, forced a smile to his lips.

"Okay, enough of this depressing talk, it's time to get on with our date. Let's agree to leave the sadness in the car, and let the fun begin. Okay?"

"Okay," I said, returning his smile.

Cal walked around and opened my door, taking my hand to help me out of the car. I felt a familiar tug in my belly at the contact. Seeing him vulnerable was breaking down my defenses.

I followed him inside, too preoccupied with

the sensations in my body to pay attention to where we were walking. The sound of Latin music made me look up, and I felt my jaw drop.

I was staring at a dance floor with a mixture of men and women, twirling and shaking their hips as they danced to the music.

"What is this?" I pulled Cal close to me and asked in his ear.

He turned to me with a big grin.

"We're going to learn Salsa dancing."

I couldn't have been more surprised if he had said that we were going to learn how to fly on a trapeze.

I let out a snort, then giggled, before pressing my hand to my mouth to try and hold it in. When Cal stopped, I tried to look up at him innocently.

"Are you laughing at my dancing abilities?" he asked sardonically.

I guffawed at that.

"What abilities?"

Cal was a notoriously bad dancer. Women ran in flocks of panic whenever he took to the dance floor.

"I can do this," he said, his face set with determination.

I reigned in my laughter.

"Sorry, of course you can."

I followed him to the dance floor, where he walked up to a woman dressed in a revealing gown and heels. He shook her hand and smiled. He must have set this up a head of time, because the woman called a man over to us, and they both turned to us with matching thousand-watt smiles.

"Are you game?" Cal turned to me and asked.

"Absolutely," I said confidently.

After a few minutes being spun around the floor by my instructor, Raul, I was less confident.

This was really hard.

I looked over at Cal and his instructor, Maria, and laughed when I saw him woodenly spinning her around.

He looked as stiff as a tin man.

Poor guy.

"At least he's trying," Raul said. "A lot of women have to come to lessons alone, because their men are afraid to look like fools."

I nodded, and looked thoughtfully at Cal. He stepped on Maria's foot and winced, but she patted his arm and kept moving.

I smiled to myself, then tried to focus on what Raul was saying.

After thirty more minutes of "training" Maria and Raul left Cal and me on the dance floor, to try and dance together.

"I'll try not to hurt you," Cal said softly. His face was red, and the sweat was causing his hair to curl up at his neck.

"I'll try not to hurt you too," I replied. "It's really hard."

Cal smiled at my words, and the pleasure on his face caused my stomach to flutter. I suddenly became aware of his hands on my hip and shoulder, skin to skin. It suddenly felt twenty degrees hotter, and when our bodies began to move together, I thought I might spontaneously combust.

I wouldn't say that we danced the Salsa well, but what we lacked in skill, we made up for in pure heat.

By the time our song ended, I saw Maria fanning herself on the sidelines. It could have just been from dancing, but I wouldn't be surprised if it was from the way Cal had watched me as we danced.

I dropped my arms and averted my eyes, afraid of the emotion that was running between the two of us. I turned on my heel and walked over to the bar to grab a glass of water.

"You okay?" Cal asked, coming up behind me.

"Yeah," I responded. "I feel like I lost a few gallons in sweat though. You want one?" I asked, indicating the bottle of water in front of me.

"Please."

I watched Maria on Raul on the dance floor as we drank. They looked absolutely amazing together.

"Wow," Cal said.

"I know, right. They're spectacular."

We watched them dance for a while longer, then Cal asked if I was ready to go.

I nodded and said, "Thanks for this, Cal. I had a lot of fun."

"Me too."

When we were on the road back to my place, I turned to him and said, "You did really well. I'm proud of you for getting out there."

Cal chuckled at that.

"It didn't start out so well, but Maria has a gift. I felt pretty good by the time we danced together. I'm glad we did it."

We sat and listened to the radio for the rest of the way. There was no awkward silence, or need to fill space with idle chatter. It felt comfortable, and I knew we were both reflecting on our date.

When he pulled up to my condo, I went to get out, but he said, "I got it," and jumped out of the car.

One of the sweetest qualities in Cal was that he was an utter gentleman. I guess I'd always taken it for granted.

I let him help me out of the car and walk me to

the door. When I turned to thank him again, I was surprised to see him walking purposefully toward me.

One second, I was standing on the step, the next I was up against the door in Cal's arms.

His hands were on my face, and his body was pressed fully against mine, I barely had time to gasp in surprise, when his mouth was on mine.

The kiss was frantic and full of need, and without a thought, I matched his need with my own. His mouth slanted over mine and our tongues met, causing a moan to escape my lips. He brought one hand around my lower back and pulled me closer to him. I lifted my leg up and assisted him as he cupped my bottom and brought me fully against him. I fisted his shirt in my hand, needing to grab on, eager to pull him closer. I nipped his bottom lip lightly, and felt a rush of cool air as he pulled his mouth away from mine.

He lowered my leg and took a step back, leaving me standing there scattered and full of need.

"I'm sorry, Shel." He leaned in and kissed my forehead lightly. "I got carried away."

Cal turned and jogged down the steps back to his car, as if he needed to get away as fast as he could.

I watched him leave with a mixture of relief

and regret before slowly turning and letting myself in.

It looked like a cold shower and a lot of soul searching was in order.

Chapter 19 - Cal

Leaving Shelly the other night had been one of the hardest things I'd ever done. The image of her flushed cheeks, and the look on her face when I'd thrust her up against the door, had made the last few nights unbearable.

I hadn't seen her since, but she didn't seemed pissed when I left, so I hoped that she was still feeling positive about us and was as eager for Saturday's date as I was.

I was waiting at a local bar and grill for TJ and Scott. We'd made plans to grab some dinner and catch half a game before Scott had to meet up with Victoria to go over wedding stuff, and TJ had to meet up with his flavor of the week to hook up.

I had no plans after dinner.

This was the highlight of my day.

How different my life had gotten in a matter of weeks. Usually, they guys were hounding me to come out and hang, and I was blowing them off to spend time at home with Shelly. Now ... I was the one who was eager for a night out, and off of Scott's couch.

This was why I was at the bar an hour earlier than our scheduled meet time, nursing a seasonal beer and munching on some chips and salsa.

I'd become a fucking loser.

"Hey, Cal," a high-pitched voice called from over my shoulder.

Shit, I thought as I recognized Melody Cannon's squeal. *Why won't this chick just leave me alone?*

"Melody," I said rather harshly, hoping she'd take a hint.

She didn't.

"You here all by your lonesome?" she asked, lifting herself onto the barstool next to mine, uninvited.

"For now," I said vaguely, turning back to my beer.

"That's a shame. You shouldn't be alone at a time like this."

I didn't take the bait; I ignored her and pretended to be caught up in the act of dipping my chip in the salsa.

"I mean," she went on as if we were having a

conversation. "What with Shelly upset with you about your ... *indiscretion*." She leaned over to me, whispering the last word, and it took every ounce of control for me not to shove her off of the stool.

I guess word had gotten out about the reason why Shelly and I were separated. I'd known it was bound to happen sooner or later, but now that Melody knew about it, it wouldn't be long before the whole town did as well.

Just what I needed.

I tried to turn farther away from her, hoping she would eventually shut up, otherwise I was going to have to walk out.

"Anyway," she continued. "I just want you to know that I'm here for you, Cal. I understand that men have needs, and I won't hold your mistakes against you."

Melody ran a finger along my arm, and I felt my body shiver in disgust. I heard her hop off of the stool and giggle.

"See you around," she said before she walked away.

I don't know how long I sat there, scowling at my beer after she left, but was startled when a strong hand clapped on my back.

"What'd that beer do to you, man?" TJ asked with a chuckle. "How long have you been here?"

I shook my head, eager to forget Melody and spend time with my buddies.

"Not that long," I answered as I stood. "Let's go grab a table."

TJ walked up to the hostess, leaned in and said something, then gave her a wink and headed back to a table in the corner with a good view of the big screen.

"You make plans with her later?" I asked with a chuckle as we sat.

"Jealousy doesn't suit you," TJ said wryly, causing me to laugh.

It was a good laugh too, the kind that starts deep in your belly. It felt really good.

We watched the TV in silence, so caught up in the game neither of us noticed when Scott walked up to the table.

"Is someone gonna move over, or am I sitting at the bar?"

I looked up sharply, surprised at Scott's tone, and then the look on his face.

He looked pissed.

I scooted over to give him some room, watching his expression as he told the waitress to grab him a whiskey on the rocks.

"Everything alright, brother?" I asked, seriously concerned. Scott didn't get ruffled very often, and he only drank whiskey when he was really pissed.

Scott just grunted and shook his head.

"Something at work?" TJ prodded.

Scott looked up at TJ, then over at me. "Nah, nothing at work."

"What is it?" I asked again.

Scott looked at me and his face lightened up a bit. He rubbed his hand across his face before replying, "It's not that big of a deal, and I hate to complain and sound like a pussy, especially with everything that you're going through right now, Cal ... But, fuck ... Victoria is driving me insane."

TJ and I shared a moment while Scott's head was down, and I knew my eyes were as wide as his were. Scott had never said anything negative to us about Victoria before. It was hard to believe, but it was the truth.

"What's going on?" I asked him, trying not to sound too excited that Victoria may finally get what she deserves.

The boot.

The waitress brought Scott's whiskey, and I motioned to her to bring me another beer, and he took a long sip before saying, "It's all of this wedding stuff. We had agreed to have a medium-sized ceremony, so that we could invite friends and family, and now she's trying to change everything. She says that she wants it to be smaller and more intimate, which is fine, but then ... "He paused and looked at us both again quickly before downing the rest of his drink.

"Then ..." TJ prodded.

"Then she said that she wants it to just be family. She doesn't want our friends to attend."

"What the fuck?" TJ asked.

"Hell, no," I said as well. "We're your boys, you can't get married without us."

"I know," Scott said, his face tightening up again. "And that's what I told her, but she threw Vegas in my face, and said that when we are all together, bad shit happens, and she wants her wedding to be perfect."

Fuck, I thought. *Now my bullshit is interfering with Scott's life.*

"Scott, man ... I'm so sorry," I stuttered, the shame burning my throat. "I understand if you need to do this without me."

Scott turned and put his hand at the back of my neck, holding me still so that I had to look directly into his very angry eyes.

"Never gonna happen, Cal," he said pointedly.

Scott let me go and stood up at the edge of the table.

"I just came by to tell you guys what was going on. Face to face. Now I have to go meet Victoria and deal with this." With that said, Scott turned and walked out the door.

"I guess I've got his drink," TJ said wryly.

I chuckled.

"It's on me, since I'm the one fucking up his life."

"Don't pull that bullshit on me, Cal. Victoria is a bitch from way back. She would have found a way to pull this shit one way or another, you're just a convenient scapegoat."

I nodded at TJ, but watched the condensation drip down my glass as I wondered if that damn night in Vegas was going to keep finding ways to fuck with me.

Chapter 20 - Shelly

I found myself looking forward to my date with Cal more and more as Saturday got closer. When Saturday finally came, I was dressed and waiting for him to ring my bell.

When it rang, signaling his arrival, I felt my belly flutter and tried to hide my grin as I opened the door.

"Hey," I said as I saw him standing before me. He looked me up and down, taking in my workout pants, shirt, and shoes with a smile.

"Ready?" he asked.

"I think so," I replied, unsure of what was to come, but excited at the possibilities.

We rode out together, and I tried to get him to say where we were going, but he kept his lips sealed, forcing me to speculate all the way there.

When we pulled into a zip-line course, I was shocked and totally taken aback.

"Seriously?" I asked when he parked by the little wooden shack.

"Yeah," Cal said, turning to me. "It'll be a blast. You'll see, Shel."

I nodded, but my stomach turned with dread, as I thought about the fact that Cal fully expected me to jump off of a platform suspended only by rope.

Oh. My. God.

I got out of the car slowly, taking in my surroundings and choking back bile as my heart beat rapidly.

I stood outside while he went inside, and followed numbly as he led me to the platform. Once there, we were corralled into a line and placed into protective gear. I winced as someone took my picture. Before I knew it I had full gear and a helmet, and I was shaking in my boots.

Literally.

We followed a group to the first platform, where I vaguely heard the guide tell us that there would be six zip-lines in all. When we got to the top, I stood and watched the others go as I waited until my turn.

It was like an out-of-body experience, and I couldn't believe that it was actually happening.

"Shelly," Cal said from the left of me, his voice traced with worry. "Are you okay, babe? We can leave if you don't want to do this."

He put his arm on my shoulder and exclaimed, "Shit! You're shaking like a leaf."I watched as a six-year-old jumped off the platform and rode the rope with a shout of glee.

"No, I'm good," I responded, trying to control my body and put my brave face on. "I can do this."

When they called for the next person, I walked to the head of the line, wanting to go before Cal, if for no other reason than I didn't want to be the last person left behind.

When I walked to the front, the guide told me to clasp my rope to the zip-line, and showed me where to keep my hands. After he checked to make everything was secure, he told me to sit down and remain seated, with my hands in place, and that they would catch me on the other end.

I sat in my holster and closed my eyes as he pushed me off the platform and I felt myself become suspended in the air. I opened my eyes and looked around, momentarily spooked by the fact that I was hanging by only ropes ... But once I realized that I was safe, I allowed myself to revel in the excitement that was coursing through my body. When I saw that I was approaching the end of the line, I placed my hand where the guide had told me I needed to in order to slow my descent. When the big guy waiting at the platform caught me, I laughed out loud.

That hadn't been so bad after all.

I turned to watch as Cal came flying down the zip-line, laughing at the look of pure glee and shout of excitement that preceded him.

My bravado wore off when I reached the next platform.

"This time, we want each of you to run and jump off," the guide explained when we were all gathered around.

I looked at Cal, my eyes big, and scowled at his grin.

"You just did this, Shel," he said encouragingly. "No worries."

"But last time they pushed me, I don't know if I can jump," I replied, explaining my fear.

"Just remember how awesome it felt when you were soaring through the air. Don't be afraid, the line will hold you."

I nodded and tried to calm my breathing as I walked to the edge.

"Ready?" the guide asked.

"Umm, hmmm," I mumbled.

"Okay, jump when you're ready."

I walked away from the edge, then turned. I ran toward the edge, but when I saw the drop off of the platform, I stopped.

"I don't think I can do this," I said softly to the guide.

"Sure you can," he replied. "Just close your eyes and jump."

I looked at him doubtfully, then turned to give it another try.

When I got to the edge, I stopped again.

"I can't," I pleaded. "Can't you just throw me again?"

The guide chuckled and shook his head.

"What if you just stand at the edge and jump off, rather than running?" he suggested.

I turned to look at Cal, who was watching me, his face etched with worry.

I didn't want to be a chicken, and I tried to convince myself that I wouldn't plunge to my death.

So I walked to the edge, closed my eyes, and jumped with a loud squeal.

Once I was airborne, and felt the security of the wire, I opened my eyes and relaxed, allowing myself to enjoy the ride.

I waited for Cal, and as we walked to the next platform, he took my hand in his.

"I'm proud of you, Shelly," Cal said as we began to climb the stairs. "You're conquering your fears. Is it horrible, or are you having a little fun? Any time you want to leave, just say the word."

I turned to him with a smile.

"It is scary, but it's also amazing. I don't want to leave."

He rewarded me with a huge smile, and when we got to the top, we found out it was a tandem jump. At least I wouldn't have to run or jump off on my own this time. I could leave the hard work to Cal.

"Can you be the one to get us off the platform?" I asked him as we waited.

"You bet," he responded, squeezing my hand.

When it was our turn to go, I eagerly wrapped my legs around Cal's, and prepared myself for the jump.

"You ready, Shel?" Cal asked with a grin of excitement.

I barely said, "Yes!" before we were flying through the air, wrapped up in each other's arms.

I took in the tree tops and expanse of land around us, then smiled broadly at Cal and said, "Thanks!"

"I knew you'd love it," Cal said, then he leaned in and nuzzled my ear.

I spent the rest of the trip down burning with the thrill of the ride and the feel of my body and Cal's tangled in each other.

I reigned in my hormones for the rest of the ride, and was excited when at the last zip-line they told us it would be a race between two lines.

"You're going down," I yelled to Cal gleefully.

"You wish," Cal responded with a laugh.

They told us that at the count of three, we were to run and jump off of the platform, then lean back to try and gain speed. The first one to the end was the winner.

I beat Cal to the finish.

We were laughing when we turned in our gear. Our adrenaline was pumping and we were both starving, so we decided to eat at the little roadside stand on the way out of the course.

Our bellies full of hot dogs, chips, and a drink, we drove the whole way back to my house talking about the different zip-line courses, and the challenges that we'd faced.

It was the most fun I'd had in weeks, and when we pulled into my driveway, I still felt the adrenaline pumping through my veins.

When Cal walked me to my door, I turned to him and asked, "Would you like to come in for a beer?"

His face looked truly happy, and I realized that it had been a long time since I'd seen him that way.

He followed me inside and I led him toward the kitchen.

"Nice place," he said.

"Thanks," I responded quietly. I didn't want to dwell on the fact that I was living in a new place on my own. I wanted to continue with the easy camaraderie that we'd had all day.

I pulled the beers out of the fridge and popped the tops, then turned to hand one to Cal. He took a long pull, then set it on the counter before turning to me and saying, "I'm sorry if this is out of line, Shel."Before I understood what he meant, I was pushed up against the counter, his lips on mine, and my legs came up around him. My bottom landed on the counter, and I groaned as his lips trailed down my neck.

"Is this okay?" Cal asked softly in my ear.

Chapter 21 – Cal

My body throbbed painfully as I waited for her answer. I nuzzled her softly under her ear, in the spot I knew would cause her to come undone.

When I heard her moan and say, "Yes," on a soft breath, I wanted to shout out in victory. Instead, I decided to show her how much I'd missed her.

I turned my mouth greedily to hers, pulling her hips closer to the edge of the counter as I brought my body to meet hers. My hands began to travel the length of her, worshiping her, as my mouth did the same.

With every hitch of her breath, I felt my body ignite and burn.

My lips traveled across her jaw and down her creamy neck as my hands found her breasts, which were full and heavy. Her nipples were taunt, and when I rubbed my palms across them, Shelly leaned farther in to me.

I felt her hands reach for the bottom of my shirt, and I leaned back far enough to allow her to pull it over my head. Her hot hands began to touch my exposed skin, and I jolted as desire whipped through me.

I tugged her shirt off quickly, then brought her to me so we were touching skin to skin.

It felt like coming home, back to the place I was always meant to be. Our bodies knew each other, and we knew how to turn each other on.

I unclasped her bra as her hands continued their assault on my chest. My breath hissed out when Shelly pinched my nipples and rolled them through her fingertips.

I put my hand at the base of her neck and fisted her hair in my hand, causing her head to fall back and giving me access to lay claim on her mouth. I kissed her greedily, my brain a haze of need, before I kissed a trail down to her succulent breasts. I took one nipple in my mouth as I fondled her other breast with my free hand. She moaned loudly, so I bit down softly, causing her to buck against my mouth.

Her responsiveness caused my dick to harden to a painful level, and I rocked my hips against hers roughly, unable to control the movement.

Able to read my body as well as I could read hers, Shelly unbuttoned my jeans and reached below the edge of my boxers to run her hand along the length of me. I felt her soft palm stroke me and my control snapped.

Before I even knew I'd managed it, I'd lifted Shelly off of the counter and was pulling her jeans off before her feet hit the floor. She lifted her feet, one by one, to allow me to slip her jeans off, but rather than standing and lifting her back up, I leaned in and kissed her.

I trailed my hands up the back of her legs, grasping her delicious ass and pulling her closer to my face. Her groans got louder as I licked and sucked, and I prayed to God that I wouldn't come right there on the floor.

I felt her hand grip my hair, urging me closer, faster, and I felt her legs tense, so I pushed my tongue inside her and nuzzled her with my nose, until her entire body began to shake around me.

When her hand went lax on my head, I stood swiftly, lifting her as I did, and placed her back on the counter. I shucked off my jeans and boxers and grasped her face, bringing her satisfied gaze to mine. She smiled languidly at me and I brought our lips together, plunging my tongue in her mouth as I slowly eased my length into her.

Jesus Christ! She felt amazing, and as she slowly took in every inch of me, clenching and surrounding me with her heat, I felt as if I was losing the ability to breathe.

When I filled her completely, her head fell back and her hips came up. I grabbed them and brought her as close to me as possible, then I began to move. What started out slow and worshipful soon turned to mind-numbing need. Shelly braced herself with one hand on the counter and the other on my shoulder while I pounded into her. When her body tensed and I felt the vibrations transfer from her body to mine, I shouted out as the most intense orgasm of my life shattered me.

I swear I blacked out for a minute. When I came to, Shelly and I were breathing rapidly, our bodies slick with sweat. My forehead was resting on her shoulder, and I pursed my lips to kiss her skin softly.

I eased myself out of her slowly, then brought my hand to her cheek and leaned in to kiss her lips. Now that the frenzy had died down, I wanted nothing more than to carry her to bed, wrap my arms around her, and kiss her all night.

When I pulled back to look in her eyes, my stomach filled with dread.

Shelly looked at me, her face full of worry and confusion.

"Shel?" I asked, terrified that she was

regretting what had just happened.

She put her hand on my chest and pushed slightly, jumping down off the counter when I moved back a step.

"Just give me a minute," she said.

I watched helplessly as she walked out of the kitchen. Not sure what I should do, I bent down and picked up our clothes. I put mine on and folded hers neatly, placing it on the counter before turning to lean against it as I waited for her to come back. I picked up my beer and took a long pull, hoping to ease the burning sensation that was building in my throat.

I hoped she was coming back.

Shit, what if she isn't coming back? I thought, before I heard her footsteps coming back down the hall.

When she entered the kitchen, she was wearing a robe and looked just as confused as she had a moment ago.

"Are you okay?" I asked, moving toward her.

She held up her hand to stop me.

"I am," she responded, but her eyes were sad when they looked at me. "I just need time to think about what happened."

"I asked if you were okay," I said, desperately. "I would have stopped ..."

"I know, Cal," she said softly. "I'm not blaming you for anything. I wanted to have sex with you, I just don't know what to do now."

"Let me stay," I said softly.

Shelly shook her head slowly. "I can't."

Chapter 22 – Shelly

"You had sex with him," Sasha said knowingly, pointing her finger at me and grinning wildly.

I looked up at her, then down at myself and asked, "What? Am I wearing a sign?"

"I can just tell," Sasha said with a shake of her hips. "How was it? Where did it happen? Tell me everything."

Sasha slid into the booth across from me and put her hands together in front of her, then looked at me and fluttered her eyelashes.

I laughed. A wonderful, deep-belly laugh.

"You're nuts," I said, trying to deflect.

"Nope," Sasha responded. "You aren't clamming up on me." She reached her hand across the table and placed it over mine, looking at me with a serious expression. "Are you okay?"

I bit my lip and nodded.

"I am. I wanted him, and I'm not sorry it happened. Shit … it was great sex. I may have seen stars, but I just don't know where to go from here."

"Where do you want to go?" Sasha asked softly.

"I don't know."

"Well, where *don't* you want to go?"

"I can't go back to the way things were, too much has happened," I began. "But I can't imagine my life without Cal in it. I just don't know in what capacity I can handle him. And, although I loved having sex with Cal, I don't want to get his hopes up, or cause him more pain. We've both been through enough in the last few weeks."

Sasha nodded and patted my hand thoughtfully. "So, 'great sex,' huh?"

I giggled at her and said, "Yeah, right there on my new kitchen counter."

"What happened on your kitchen counter?" Gaby asked as she slid in next to me. "Coffee, please," she said to the cute waiter who eyed her appreciatively.

"Shelly and Cal had mind-altering sex on it," Sasha explained.

Gaby's mouth dropped open and she turned slowly to look at me.

"What? When? How?" she sputtered slowly.

I waited for the waiter to serve Gaby's coffee before answering her.

"We went zip-lining for our fourth date. It was terrifying, and amazing, and totally exhilarating. I don't know, maybe our adrenaline was pumping in overdrive, or maybe I was just horny, but I invited him inside when we got back to my place, and I'd barely given him his beer before he had me up against the counter."

"Oh my," Sasha said, fanning herself dramatically.

"Go on …" Gaby encouraged.

"He gave me the opportunity to stop it, but I didn't want to. I wanted him so much I could barely stand it. Once we were done, reality sunk back in, and he asked me to let him stay."

"Did you?" Gaby asked.

I shook my head.

"No, I couldn't. I know that Cal wants our relationship to be the way it was, and I knew that if I allowed him to stay, I'd just hurt him more in the long run."

"So, you still plan on going through with the divorce?" Sasha asked, her voice tinged with sadness.

"I can't forget what he did, Sash. And as much as I miss him, I can't give him false hope. I still plan to go through with the divorce. Maybe I should put a stop to this eight weeks thing. I don't know if either of us can handle another month of dates."

We all sat quietly at the table, lost in thought, until the waiter came back and asked us if we were ready to order.

Once our order was in, I sighed deeply and asked, "Please, can we talk about something else? I need one of you to tell me something that is going to get my mind off of everything that I have going on in my life."

"Hmmm ... I slept with a hot guy I was showing a house to ... in the house I was showing him," Sasha said with a saucy wink, causing me to laugh.

"That's not news," I teased her. "That's a regular day in your world."

"True," Sasha conceded.

We both turned to Gaby, who looked at us nervously.

"Wow, you look like you really have something on your mind," I said to her. "Is everything okay?"

"Scott and I had sex," Gaby said, shocking me to the core.

"What?" Sasha and I yelled at the same time.

"Shhh," Gaby said, looking pointedly around

the restaurant. "I don't mean now … I mean in the past. We had sex on prom night."

"What?" I asked again, totally confused.

"You're saying that the two of you had sex in *high school*, and you never said anything?" Sasha asked.

Gaby nodded.

"You didn't tell us, and there is no way he told Cal or TJ, or we would all know," I said, working it out. "But why would you keep it a secret? Was it only that one night?"

"You guys had different dates to the prom," Sasha stated.

"Yes, we did," Gaby agreed. "And, yes, it was just the one night. We kept it a secret because we didn't want to mess up our friendship, or our group dynamics."

"But, how did it happen?" I asked.

The waiter chose that moment to come back to the table with our food. Gaby looked up at him and said, "Can I have a mimosa please?"

"Make that mimosas all around," Sasha added. When he walked away, Sasha turned back and waved her hand at Gaby, encouraging her to continue.

"I had a crush on Scott from the moment we met the guys junior year. He was my total opposite

... The way he was raised, and his plans for his future, but I thought he was the greatest guy I'd ever met. And hot, totally, totally hot," Gaby explained with a blush.

"You did?" I asked. "How come you never told us?"

"I don't know," Gaby admitted. "I guess I thought he was out of my league, and then we started hanging out all of the time because of you and Cal. Then, after a while, we were all inseparable, and he was one of my best friends, I was afraid to ruin it. Plus, when he wasn't hanging out with us, he was always with some girl. Scott was never lonely, and I didn't feel like I could compete."

"That's ridiculous," Sasha said angrily. "You're amazing! Any guy who comes into a five-foot radius of you is ready to fall at your feet. Scott isn't out of your league. Don't sell yourself short."

"How did you guys end up hooking up?" I asked, eager to learn this secret that two of my best friends had managed to keep from us for the last six years.

"Well, you know we all hung out at the prom together, but what you don't know is that after you guys left to go to your hotel rooms, I realized that Tom was not the guy that I wanted to lose my virginity too. I tried to explain that I wasn't going to go with him to the hotel, and let him down easy, but he didn't take it well. Scott was walking by with his date, and saw Tom grab my arm. Before I knew it, he had Tom up against the wall and had his hand around Tom's throat."

"What?" Sasha asked, shocked. "You never told us any of this."

Gaby nodded and continued, "I calmed Scott down enough to get him to let Tom go, but I was pretty shaken up. Scott left his date to take me to his room so that I could calm down. Boy, was she pissed," Gaby said with a laugh. She had a small smile on her face as her memories took her back to that night.

"It started out innocently enough. We talked and had a few drinks, and I thanked him for helping me out … Apologized for ruining his night. He said I hadn't, and after a few of those drinks, I began to feel bold. I told him that I'd had a crush on him, and he said that he felt the same. We started kissing, and one thing led to another."

"Oh my God!" I exclaimed, bringing my hand to my lips, my heart filled with emotion. "You lost your virginity to Scott …"

"We both did," Gaby said, that smile still on her lips. "It was his first time too."

"What?" Sasha asked. "Scott didn't have sex

until prom? What about all of those girls throughout high school?"

"He said he never went all the way with them. He wanted it to mean something," Gaby explained.

"That's so beautiful," I said softly, my eyes tearing.

"What are you getting so emotional about?" Gaby asked with a laugh.

"The two of you. Two of my best friends. What a beautiful story. I can't believe you guys kept this from us this whole time. Why didn't you pursue a relationship after that?" I asked.

"Like I said, we didn't want to ruin our relationship, or mess up the group. Plus, I was going to culinary school, and he was going away to study business ... The timing wasn't right. Then, it seemed like one of us was always dating someone, so it never worked out."

"Did you want it to?" Sasha asked.

"Yes," Gaby admitted sadly. "I never stopped wanting him. That's why I'm telling you guys this now. I don't know what to do ... Scott is about to make a big mistake and marry that horrible woman."

Sasha and I nodded in agreement; none of us had an ounce of love for Victoria.

"What do you want to do?" Sasha asked.

"I want to stop him," Gaby responded.

Chapter 23 – Cal

"I had sex with Shelly," I said quietly, so only Scott and TJ could hear me. We were in the bleachers at the high school, waiting for Craig's opening game to start. We'd gotten there early to get good seats, but people were starting to fill in around us, and I didn't want anyone to overhear my words, least of all my mother, who was sitting in the bleachers above us.

"That's great, man," TJ said with a grin as he took a bite of his loaded hot dog.

Scott made a face at TJ, then turned to me seriously and asked, "How'd that go?"

"It was rough," I admitted softly. "I mean, the sex was fantastic, but afterwards …"

"What happened?" TJ asked around a mouth full of food.

Scott hit him in the arm and asked, "What happened?"

"Ow," TJ protested, then took another bite.

"It turned awkward," I replied. "I wanted to stay, you know … Talk stuff out and sleep over, but she didn't want me to. She said she couldn't handle it."

"What are you complaining about?" TJ asked. "Sex without having to cuddle afterwards … That's the best."

Scott hit him again.

"Do that one more time, bro, and I'm hitting back."

"This is my wife, TJ, not some one-night stand. I'm not looking for a quick lay, I'm trying to get my marriage back." My voice began to rise as I finished my sentence, and my mom cleared her throat behind us, indicating that she could hear us. "Just forget about it," I spat out.

"Cal, I'm sorry, man, you know I didn't mean it like that," TJ replied. "You and Shelly are gonna work it out."

Scott nodded and clapped me on the back. "You're gonna get her back."

The game was starting, so we turned to the field.

I stood up and clapped, shouting as Craig rounded the bases after hitting a triple.

"He's so good," Scott said with a grin as he put his fingers to his lips and let out a shrill whistle.

"Yeah, he's going to go far," I said with pride. "He's not destined to be a grease monkey, I can tell you that."

"Hey," TJ responded. "Nothing wrong with turning a wrench."

"Shit, I know that, but it's not the most dependable way to earn a living," I said wryly. TJ made a face and took a pull of his root beer.

Our shop was in a bit of a slump. We weren't getting as many appointments as usual, and walk-in business hadn't been good. It looked like we were about to get fewer hours, which wasn't good news for TJ or myself.

"Speaking of which, you remember my buddy Brock?" TJ asked.

"From the west side store?" I asked. TJ had started out years ago at a store on the other side of town, before he'd moved to work in the shop with me.

"Yeah," TJ confirmed. "He left a couple years ago and started his own painting business. It's been going pretty good. He said if I needed the cash, he could bring me in for some jobs. I'm gonna start next week. If you're interested, I can throw your name in."

I'd never been a painter, but if we were losing hours at the shop, I'd need to pick up a paycheck wherever I could. "Sounds good, thanks."

"Brock is the dude that was hitting on Gaby at the New Year's Party a couple years back, right? The stupid masquerade one at the bar?" Scott asked with a frown.

"Yup, that's him," TJ said with a chuckle. "Dude is smooth with the ladies."

I remembered the party that Scott was talking about. Shelly and I had gone dressed in all black, with black masks. Scott was right, it had been a ridiculous party theme, but the girls had liked it, and Shelly looked totally hot. We'd ended up sneaking into the backroom and having sex on the manager's desk. I smiled at the memory. I also remembered how much Brock had seemed to piss Scott off that night.

I turned to ask him about it, but the sound of my mom going crazy behind me had me turning to the field instead. I looked up in time to see the ball Craig had hit sail over the fence, and see his grin as he jogged slowly around the bases.

My mom was going apeshit. I turned to her with a laugh and said, "Calm down, Killer, you're going to embarrass him."

My mom turned to me, her face flush with pleasure, and said, "Oh … Shush." Then she started clapping and screaming Craig's name even louder.

I laughed at her exuberance, and joined in the cheering.

Once we'd calmed down, I nudged Scott and asked, "Hey, I remember that night. You and Brock seemed to get off on the wrong foot. What was that about?"

Scott kept his eyes on the game and replied, "Nothing. I just thought he was an ass. No big deal. It was a long time ago."

"An ass?" TJ asked, surprised. "Brock is one of the most laid-back guys I know. I don't remember you guys even talking that night. He's a good dude."

Scott shrugged and said, "Like I said, it was a long time ago. I'm sure he's cool."

I wondered what the real issue was. Scott wasn't usually quick to judge, and he was a pretty easygoing guy himself. Usually got along with everyone. Maybe if TJ and I started working with Brock, we'd invite him to hang out sometime. I was sure that he and Scott would get along great, if they just took a minute to get to know each other.

I glanced at TJ. He looked like he was relaxed and enjoying the game, but I knew the troubles at the shop were getting to him. Not only did he love working there, but he lived in a little apartment off the back of it, so if things got as bad as the boss had implied and the place closed for a while, TJ was worried that he'd not only be out of a job, but that he'd also be out of a place to live.

TJ'd been raised by his grandparents, and they'd both passed away about a year before. They hadn't had money, and the house they'd lived in for their fifty-plus years of marriage had been mortgaged to the hilt, and TJ hadn't been able to save it. Stability was very important to TJ now, since he'd never had it as a child, and I really hoped that our boss was going to be able to keep his business afloat … for TJ's sake. Yeah, I was worried about keeping the job myself, but TJ had worked hard to be where he was now, and I hated to think of him being forced to take a step back.

"You good?" Scott asked, pulling me out of my thoughts.

"Yeah, brother," I responded with a smile.

"Craig's got a gift, man," TJ said when Craig made a double play.

"That he does," I replied, and I was going to everything in my power to make sure he took advantage of that gift.

Chapter 24 – Shelly

"Shit!" I exclaimed when my truck began to slow down to a stop, barely giving me enough time to pull over to the side of the road. I slapped the steering wheel with my hands and groaned.

I was going to be late for work.

I looked around the car, helpless, as if surveying the interior would give me some idea as to what went wrong.

I knew next to nothing about cars. I was married to a mechanic, it had never been something I'd had to worry about. Cal always took care of it for me.

I picked up my cell and dialed Sasha, without bothering to look at the time. Gaby had to be to the bakery early every morning, so I knew she'd already be at work. I had a better chance of catching Sasha.

"Hello?" a male voice said over the line.

I pulled the phone away from my ear to look

at the display. It said Sasha.

"Hello, is Sasha there?" I asked.

"Uh … Yeah," came the reply. The sound became muffled, so I assumed he placed his hand over the speaker.

"You Sasha?" I heard him ask.

I put my hand over my mouth to contain my laugh when I heard her reply, "You bet. Give me the phone, big guy."

"Shel?" Sasha said sleepily when she got her phone.

"Hey, Sash, I hate to bother you," I said with a barely repressed giggle. "But something's wrong with my car. Do you think you could come get me?"

"I'll be there in ten," she replied.

I gave her the cross streets and hung up.

I loved Sasha more than I could ever say, but I never understood how she could handle the casual relationships she had with men.

I'd always been a one-man woman.

Whereas Sasha made sure that no man was ever around long enough to matter. The only people she let in were Gaby, Cal, TJ, Scott, and me.

She'd moved around a lot as a kid. Her parents were big in the world of fashion, so she'd spent her childhood all around the globe. Paris, Florence, England. When her parents divorced, she'd moved here with her father, and begged him to let her stay here to finish out high school. He had, but he'd never been around much. Sasha had been mostly left with the housekeepers, but at least she'd gotten to stay and graduate with us. Her dad moved soon after she graduated, but he'd bought her a townhouse, and she'd stayed.

Although Gaby and I always envied the places Sasha had gotten to see, Sasha always envied the fact that we had been born and raised here.

I was startled out of my thoughts by a knock on the window. Sasha managed to look fabulous, even with no makeup and her hair pulled back and covered by a hat.

I opened the door and got out, grabbing her in a hug before pulling back to say, "Thank you!"

"No problem, I needed that guy to hit the road anyway," Sasha replied with a grin. "Hey, I knew you wouldn't want me to call Cal, so I called TJ ..."

"You did?" I asked with a frown. TJ was just going to run and tell Cal. I wondered if he would be upset that I didn't call him.

"Yeah, I'm sorry, but you know I'm even more inept than you when it comes to cars. Do you want to wait for TJ, or do you want me to take you to work?"

"I'll wait," I said with a sigh. "So, who was the guy?"

"The guy I was telling you about the other day, the one I sold the house to," Sasha said with a shrug.

"Again?" I asked, surprised. "What's his name?"

"Sean," Sasha replied. "But don't get your hopes up, it's no big deal."

I nodded, but I couldn't help but get my hopes up a little bit. I wanted Sasha to settle down and be happy. I just wasn't sure if she would allow herself to.

At the sound of a car coming up the street, we both looked up. TJ's latest salvage, a beat-up old El Camino, came rolling up to a stop behind us.

"Where did you get that piece of shit?" Sasha asked when TJ got out of the car.

"Woman, this fine piece of machinery is a classic," TJ said with a grin, running his hand along the hood as he walked toward us. "When I get her fixed up, I'll let you take her for a spin, and I guarantee you'll eat your words."

Sasha didn't reply, just watched him walk toward us with narrowed eyes.

TJ stopped in front of us and pushed his sunglasses up to the top of his head before giving Sasha a wicked grin. "Got an itch that needs scratchin', Red?"

"Nope," Sasha said with a popping sound on the p. "I've already had a *real* man take care of that for me this mornin'."

TJ just gave her a wink, then turned to me, all traces of humor gone, and asked, "What seems to be the problem, babe?"

"I don't know," I admitted, feeling like a first-class idiot. "It just stopped working."

TJ held out his hand and I dropped the keys in it, stepping back to give him access to the truck. He opened the door and sat down, putting the key in the ignition and turning it slightly. I looked over at Sasha when TJ got out of the truck, eyes bright and looking like he was trying not to laugh.

"What?" I asked.

"When's the last time you put gas in it?" he asked with a chuckle.

"No ..." I said softly, mortification slowly taking over.

Sasha let out a bark of laughter, and before I knew it, we were all bent over laughing.

"Shit, Shel, even I know to put gas in the tank," Sasha said, tears forming in her eyes.

"Shut up," I managed to yell between breaths. "Cal always took care of everything with my truck."

"Even the gas?" TJ asked incredulously.

I nodded, bringing my hand to my side as it began to cramp.

"Wow, that boy really was whipped," Sasha said with a giggle.

I sobered instantly, suddenly feeling stupid and ridiculous. What was I doing? How was I going to move forward and get through life if I couldn't even fill up my own tank?

TJ's arm came up around my shoulder, and he pulled me to his side. "I gotcha, Shel. I have a gas can in my trunk. I'll run and get some gas and we'll get you to work in no time."

I nodded and put my arm around him, pulling him close for a half hug. "Thanks."

When he pulled away, Sasha wiped her face and said, "I'm sorry. I didn't mean to make you feel bad."

I shook my head. "No, it's not your fault. It's stupid that I didn't think of it."

"Hey," she said, putting her finger under my chin so I was forced to look her in the eye. "You aren't stupid. You're just trying to figure out how to be on your own. You guys were together for six years, Shelly. It's going to take some time. Don't be so hard on yourself."

I smiled up at her, but couldn't help but wonder … When was it going to get easier?

Chapter 25 – Cal

I'd been planning this night since before our anniversary. It was the gift I was going to give Shelly, but hadn't had the chance to. I bought floor seats to the Hunter Hayes concert. She was going to freak out. I couldn't wait to see the look on her face. The look I should have seen on our anniversary, before I'd ruined everything.

I'd been thinking about our last date every night since. I couldn't get Shelly out of my mind. Now that I'd had a taste of her again, I was more determined than ever to convince her that we had to be together.

When I pulled up to her place, I thought back to what TJ said yesterday afternoon at work.

"You guys love each other, bro. I've never seen a couple that belongs together the way that you do, you just have to keep doing what you're doing, and have faith … I do."

I ignored the nerves that were pounding through me and walked to the door.

When Shelly answered my knock, I was rendered momentarily speechless.

Her hair was fluffed out in a way that made it frame her face perfectly. Her eyes were smoky, her lips red, and the diamond stud flashed in the light. I let my eyes travel down, taking in her tight jeans, cowboy boots, and black halter top.

"Wow!" I said when I finally regained the ability to speak. I leaned in and kissed her on the cheek, inhaling the exquisite scent of her perfume, my body instantly turning rock hard.

"Thanks," she said with a smile and flush of pleasure.

"You ready?" I asked, offering her my arm.

Shelly locked up, then linked her arm in mine. "Yup. Where are we going?"

"A concert," I answered with a grin.

"Really?" she asked, excitement filling her voice. My girl loved concerts.

"Wait … Hunter Hayes is in town," she squealed. "Is that where we're going?"

I nodded with a grin, pleasure filling me when she jumped up and down on the sidewalk.

Nothing made me feel as good as seeing Shelly totally excited. It didn't take concerts and trips, either; little things gave her pleasure. It was one of the things I loved best about her.

Shelly chattered excitedly all the way to the stadium. I listened to her with a smile, happy that I was able to take her mind off of everything she'd been dealing with, that we both had been dealing with, and give her a night to let her hair down and do something she loves.

We grabbed a couple beers and made our way down to our seats.

"Wow," Shelly exclaimed when we found them. "These are great seats. They must have cost you a pretty penny."

Her face looked worried at that, but I squeezed her hand and leaned in to say, "Don't worry about it, Shel. Just enjoy the concert."

She nodded and looked into my eyes, her mouth forming a big grin. "Okay."

Shelly leaned in and kissed me lightly on the lips before pulling back and saying, "Thank you."

I didn't say anything, but turned and faced the stage as my heart pounded painfully in my chest. I was suddenly overtaken by fear. Terrified that I was only going to get four more weeks with Shelly until she was no longer mine to touch, hold, or kiss.

Music began to play and I tried to shake the bad feelings off, and although I was able to enjoy the show, I couldn't completely shake those traces of fear.

When Hunter Hayes came out to do his encore, I turned to watch Shelly, as I had throughout the show. She was on her feet, singing along, and smiling broadly. When Hunter sang about wanting crazy love, Shelly turned and her eyes caught mine. She kept her eyes on mine, and I saw them begin to fill with tears, so I got to my feet and took her in my arms. She held on as though her life depended on it, and we rocked together slowly to the music.

When the song ended, I pulled back enough to wipe the tears off her face. We didn't say anything. I moved my hand down to take her hand in mine, and led her out of the stadium.

When we were in the car, waiting in line for the traffic to exit the stadium, I asked, "Did you have fun?"

"Yes," Shelly said, a smile once more on her face. I wanted to keep it there. "He's so good live. Thanks again."

"No problem," I answered.

We sat there for a few minutes, not saying anything, and not moving more than an inch. Finally I turned to her and asked, "Hey, my family's having a get-together for Craig's eighteenth birthday. Dinner and stuff, nothing major, just the family, and I was wondering if you'd go with me."

"Do you think that's a good idea?" Shelly asked. "I mean, your parents know about us, right?"

"Yeah, but I don't think anyone's said anything to Craig, and you know he loves you." It was probably dirty of me to use my brother to get Shelly to spend extra time with me, but I was willing to use whatever I had at my disposal.

I could tell by Shelly's face that it worked. "Of course, when is the dinner?"

"It's on Wednesday night, on his birthday," I answered. "I think he's doing stuff with his friends to celebrate over the weekend."

"I can't believe he's eighteen already," Shelly said. "It seems like just yesterday he was turning thirteen and we were celebrating at the bowling alley. Do you remember that?"

"Yeah," I said with a smile as I remembered my brother and I watching Shelly try to bowl. We'd had a good laugh over the way she'd stomp her foot whenever she'd bowled a gutter ball. Craig had always been a little in love with Shelly himself. "I can't believe he's about to graduate. Time goes by quickly."

"It sure does," Shelly replied softly. "Hey, speaking of the past … You are not going to believe what Gaby told me and Sasha today."

"What's that?" I asked, wondering if we were ever going to get out of this parking lot.

"She and Scott lost their virginity to each other."

I forgot about the traffic, turning to Shelly with my mouth open. "Get the fuck out of here."

Shelly laughed and shook her head. "I can't … It's true."

"When? How? Why didn't they tell us?" I asked, my mind totally blown.

"It was prom night," Shelly answered.

"Shit, I knew that Scott lost his virginity on prom night, but he never said it was with Gaby. How the hell did that happen?" "I guess Scott walked by when Gaby was telling Tom that she wanted to go home instead of to the hotel, and when Tom put his hands on her, Scott got rough with him."

"Tom put his hands on her?" I asked, seeing red, even though there was absolutely nothing I could do about it now.

"Yeah, but Scott took care of it, then dropped his date in order to take care of Gaby, like the total sweetheart that he is … Anyway, after a few drinks they both admitted to having crushes on each other, and one thing led to another …"

"Wow," I said, trying to wrap my head

around this new information. "Scott and Gaby … Why did they never date each other?"

"She said that they were both about to leave for school, and that after that, one of them was always with someone else, so the timing was never right."

"That's too bad," I said. Now that I knew about them, the two of them together made perfect sense. I remembered the conversation I'd had with the guys about Brock. "I bet that's why Scott didn't like Brock … He was hitting on Gaby."

"What?" Shelly asked.

"The guys and I were talking at Craig's game the other night, and TJ mentioned that he was going to pick up some work with Brock at his painting company, and Scott said he'd thought he was an ass, but they only met once … At that New Year's masquerade we all went to."

"That was a great night!" Shelly remembered with a smile. "I do remember Brock hitting on Gaby, but she was dating that Roger guy at the time."

"It explains Scott's attitude toward Brock. I can't believe they had a one-night stand though, that's crazy … I'm gonna give Scott some shit for this!"

"You can't," Shelly exclaimed, putting her hand on my arm as if to hold me back. "If you say something to Scott, he will know Gaby told us, and Gaby will know I told you. She'll be pissed."

"Why'd you tell me?" I asked, turning to look into her eyes.

"You know I always tell you everything," Shelly answered simply.

I couldn't stop the smile that I knew took over my whole face.

Chapter 26 – Shelly

I couldn't believe how nervous I was. I mean, Cal's family is my family, but I hadn't seen them since before Vegas. I was nervous that they would treat me differently, and would be upset that I was planning to divorce their son.

I wonder if he told them that I was.

I probably should have asked him what *exactly* his parents knew, before I'd said I'd meet him at their place for Craig's birthday.

I stood on the front porch and smoothed my hand across the floral-print sundress I was wearing, trying to calm the nerves that were fluttering furiously beneath the surface.

I raised my hand to knock, then shook my head and opened the door instead. I hadn't knocked on this door for six years, it was silly of me to feel like I had to now.

I opened the door and smiled at the sounds

and smells that greeted me.

I walked up to where Craig and Scott were talking in the living room. Although Cal had said this would be a family-only dinner, I'd known that Scott would be included. He was just like another brother to Cal and Craig. Rose, Cal's mom, had always treated him just like her own boys. She'd even grounded him the weekend she found him and Cal sneaking beer from the fridge when we were all still in high school.

"Hey, birthday boy," I said with a smile when Craig turned around. He enfolded me into a hug, and I was struck by how much he looked like Cal had at eighteen.

"Not a boy anymore," Craig replied with a devilish grin. I could only imagine how the girls at school responded to that grin on the same handsome face as those amazing eyes.

I chuckled and turned to give Scott a hug. "Hey," I said smiling up into his face.

He looked a little stressed around the eyes. "Hey," Scott replied. "I'm glad you came."

I just nodded, eager to keep this night about Craig's celebration, and not about mine and Cal's relationship.

"There's my favorite girl." I looked up and watched Rose maneuver toward me from the kitchen. "Aren't you a sight for sore eyes." She turned and smacked Scott on the arm, "Don't just stand there, go get Shelly a drink … And help Cal set the table."

"Haha … I get a pardon cause it's my birthday," Craig yelled out after Scott.

"Just for that, you can go help your dad with the projector," Rose said with an arch of her eyebrow.

I stifled a giggle at the forlorn look on Craig's face as he turned to walk down the hall.

"Birthdays used to mean special privileges," Craig said to no one in particular as he walked.

Rose and I both laughed, and I felt my heart lurch as she tucked her arm in mine.

"Let's walk a bit before dinner," she said.

I nodded and followed her lead out the door.

Once we were outside, Rose didn't waste any time getting to the point.

"Shelly … Cal told me about what happened, and I am sorrier than I can ever explain, for you … and my son. I can't begin to understand the hurt and betrayal that you must have felt … must still feel … I can only imagine. And I understand that your first instinct is to cut and run, but Shelly, I have to tell you, I'm really hoping that you won't."

We both stopped and turned to look at each

other. I knew and respected Rose enough to let her finish what she felt she needed to say, but a part of me was burning inside, and I wanted to tell her to mind her own business.

But I didn't.

"Cal has loved you since the moment he saw you in that gymnasium, and as much as Harry and I worried that you kids were getting too serious too young, Cal never wavered. He told me the summer after you met that you were the girl for him, and that he would marry you as soon as he could. And he did. My son may have made a horrible mistake, but I know his heart as well as you do, and we both know that he loves you with a passion, and he always will. All I'm asking is that you take into consideration the past six years of your life, as well as that one night, before you make a final decision. I also want you to know that I love you dearly, and that no matter what decision you *do* end up making, you will always be my daughter."

I choked back a sob as my eyes filled, and we smiled at each other through our tears. I pulled her into a hug, and we both stood there for a moment, crying silently and holding on to each other.

I loved this woman dearly ... No, I loved this *family* dearly, and the thought of not having them in my life was like an added weight on my shoulders. I felt it crushing me and I wanted nothing more than to be able to get out from under it.

Suddenly, my body felt coiled with frustration and rage.

I wished whole-heartedly that Cal had never went to Vegas and fucked up our lives. His indiscretion was affecting everyone around us and I wanted to rail at him for being such an idiot.

Rose and I walked silently back to the house, and I tried to tamper down the feelings of anger. I don't know if she felt the change in me, but she patted me on the shoulder and smiled before leaving me standing on the front porch.

I breathed in and out deeply, trying to release the anger that had flooded me so completely.

"Everything okay?" I looked up just as Cal stepped out onto the porch. "I saw Mom come back in alone, so I wanted to check on you."

I looked up at him and saw my worry reflected back at me. I knew he could tell that I was upset, but didn't want to ruin the evening.

"I'm fine," I responded. "Can you come by my place later though, so we can talk?"

"Of course," Cal said with a frown. "Look, Shelly, if it's too much for you to be here, I understand. I can tell everyone you didn't feel well or something, and stop by later."

"No, that's okay," I replied, gesturing for him to lead the way back inside. "I want to be here for Craig ... I'll be okay."

We both walked quietly back inside, and I knew it was going to be a difficult meal for both of us. I just hoped we could put on brave faces for his family.

Chapter 27 – Cal

I always loved spending time with my family, the way we joked with each other, the love that was always in the room, and the laughter that inevitably filled the house. But sitting through dinner tonight was unbearable.

I was so apprehensive, worried about what Shelly wanted to talk about. I mean, I had a good idea of what she wanted to talk about, but it was the first time since we started our dates that she seemed to want to. I couldn't help but be worried about what she wanted to say. I only hoped that she wasn't going to try and back out of the last three dates.

I needed that time …

I knew that at this point, Shelly wasn't ready to forgive me or change her mind about wanting a divorce, and I couldn't handle the thought of her giving up without giving me the shot we'd agreed upon.

I physically, and emotionally, could not handle even the thought …

I tried to smile and laugh with everyone, but I knew my mom was watching Shelly and me carefully. Especially after she came back inside after talking to Shelly. I wondered what they'd had to say to each other, and my imagination was rampant with possibilities.

Scott could tell something was wrong too, and when we went to the kitchen to put candles on the cake, he pulled me to the side.

"Everything alright, bro?"

"I don't know," I whispered to him. It always seemed like my mom heard everything, and I didn't want her coming in the kitchen to batter me with questions. "Shelly asked me to come by later to talk."

Scott clapped his hand on my shoulder.

"Let me know if you need anything, and try not to let your anxiety show …"

"I was trying not to," I countered.

"Well, your acting sucks," Scott replied as he lit the candles. "Don't quit your day job."

That got a real grin out of me, so I whispered, "Asshole," as I carried the cake out, which earned me a glare from my mother.

Once the cake was devoured, we didn't have to stay long, because Craig had made plans to meet up with some of his friends. So, Shelly and I made our goodbyes rather quickly, and after promising my mother that I'd come by in the next few days, I followed Shelly to her house.

I didn't jump right out of the car after I parked; instead, I took a few minutes to try and calm my nerves. I looked up and saw Shelly waiting for me at the door, "Quit being such a pussy," I muttered to myself, then took a deep breath and got out of the car.

I followed her wordlessly into the house, and back into the kitchen. She motioned toward the table, so I walked over and grabbed a seat.

I wondered momentarily if I'd ever see any part of the house other than the kitchen.

"I'm so mad at you," Shelly said softly. The sound of raw pain in her voice made my stomach clench. She sat and looked at me, her face shuttered. "I need you to tell me everything that happened that night."

I looked at her for a moment, wanting to make sure she was sure that this was what she wanted. When I met her stony glare, I took a deep breath and began to recount that night in Vegas.

"We started at the craps table. We spent a lot of money and had a lot of free drinks in about an hour. We skipped dinner. I don't think we meant to, it just kind of happened. We went from Bellagio to Paris, and then took a cab to the other side of the strip. We would stop and gamble and have some drinks, and then we ended up going to a club.. I guess it was the lack of food and the insane amount of shots we did at the club that really fucked me up. Once we said that we were celebrating Scott's bachelor party, everyone was buying us shots. I was trashed before midnight."

I paused, my stomach in turmoil and my palms starting to sweat, but Shelly just sat there watching me silently, almost as if she was trying to separate herself emotionally from the conversation, so I continued on.

"I remember telling the guys I had to go, and they kept ragging on me, calling me a pussy, a lightweight, and whatever else they could think of to try and get me to stay, but I was too fucked up to care. They said they got me in a cab, and told the driver where we were staying. They even gave him some cash … I don't know. I don't remember anything from that point on." I wrung my hands and stared into Shelly's eyes, which were starting to tear up.

"When I woke up, I was naked and in bed with the worst hangover I'd ever had. I couldn't make it to the bathroom, so I puked in a trash can by the desk in the room. I don't know how long I threw up, but I heard the toilet flush and looked up, expecting to see one of the guys walk out, but it wasn't one of the guys."

"What did she look like?" Shelly asked, her voice barely above a whisper.

"Shelly ... it doesn't matter," I said, desperate for her to stop. I didn't want to hurt her more than I already had.

"It matters to me," she replied. "What did she look like?"

"She was blonde. Tall and blonde," I responded, my voice laced with regret.

"Where did you meet her?"

"I don't know."

"But you had sex with her."

"I don't know, Shel."

"Maybe you didn't have sex with her then, if you can't remember," Shelly asked, and I got a glimpse of hope through the tears that were falling down her face.

"We were both naked, Shelly. And although I don't remember meeting her or having sex with her, it's the only logical conclusion that I can come up with." I was sure my face reflected the regret that was filling my heart.

"So we'll never know ... Not for sure," she

surmised sadly.

I reached out my hands to hers, then took them back when she flinched.

"No," I replied softly, although my entire being wanted to scream out loud.

It was like we were back to square one. Back to the night of our anniversary, like the last five weeks didn't matter. I was crushing Shelly all over again. "I don't think I'll ever know for sure."

Shelly nodded, then brought her hands up to wipe her face.

"I need you to go now."

My heart dropped, and I wanted nothing more than to take her in my arms and hold her until both of our hearts were whole again.

"Shelly, please ..." I started, but the look on her face stopped me. I stood up, but stopped and asked before leaving, "Will you still see me on Saturday?"

"I'll let you know," she replied, then brought her haunted gaze to mine. "I'm so mad at you," she said again.

"I know," I replied. "I'm sorry."

Chapter 28 – Shelly

"What do you think?" I asked Sasha, pushing my shirt up my arm to show off my new tattoo. *Strength* was written in script across the inside of my left bicep.

"That looks wicked!" Sasha said, running her finger gently along the script. "I'm so sorry I couldn't go with you and Gaby. There was no other time I could show that house, and I really wanted the commission."

"How'd it go?" I asked as I moved up in line. We were waiting at the local deli to order our lunch. They had a killer Greek salad.

"I got it," Sasha said with a beautiful grin. She looked gorgeous with her red hair pulled back into a high ponytail and wearing a sophisticated, yet sexy, gray pinstripe suit.

"'Atta girl," I replied, putting my hand up for a high five.

I stepped up to the register to put in my order, then shifted to the side to wait for Sasha to put in hers.

I glanced up when the door jangled, signaling someone's entrance to the deli, and my heart fluttered when I saw it was Cal.

I took advantage of the fact that he hadn't yet noticed me, and I looked him over slowly.

He had always been the hottest guy I'd ever seen.

He still was …

He was dressed for work, so he had stains of grease scattering his clothes, and his hands had streaks of gray … Like he'd tried to wash up, but hadn't had time to get his hands totally free of grease. I'd always thought he'd looked hot when he was working. Some people may be turned off by the mess, but not me. I'd always loved knowing that Cal was a strong, capable man who could make something that was broken, whole again.

His hair was mussed, like he'd spent the better part of the day running his hands through it, and his face was dark with the shadow of a day-old beard.

As I watched him, my body became flushed and aware, as if it was attuned to the fact that my mate was in the vicinity.

"Shit," Sasha said from behind me, causing me

to jump. "You're making me horny … You're looking at Cal like he's on the menu, and you're starved."

"Shut up," I hissed at her, but she just chuckled and yelled out, "Hey, Cal!"

I shot her a look that I hoped conveyed that I wanted to chop her into bits, then turned and smiled as Cal walked over.

"Hey, Shel … Sasha," Cal said when he got close enough for us to hear him. "I'm just picking up lunch for TJ and me, how's it going?"

He had a smile on his face, but his eyes looked troubled as they searched my face.

Things hadn't ended well after Craig's birthday, and I hadn't contacted him yet to let him know whether I still wanted to go out Saturday or not. I'd been able to think of little else … but it seemed like our relationship is all I've thought about and I still had no idea what to do about it.

I loved Cal, and I probably always would, but I didn't know if I could continue to be his wife … And I didn't know if I could continue giving him hope.

"I'm gonna go to the bathroom," Sasha said suddenly, walking off quickly to give Cal and me privacy, her heels tapping across the linoleum as she did.

"How's it going?" I asked.

"How've you been?" Cal asked at the same time.

We both chuckled nervously, him looking toward the register, while I looked around the room, neither of us meeting each other's eyes.

"I'm sorry about the other night," I said softly, running my hand through my hair with a sigh.

"Hey, what's that?" he asked, his hand coming up to touch the beginning of my tattoo.

I lifted my sleeve up to show him the word, then pulled it back down.

"Tattoo," I responded.

"I like it," Cal said, his eyes still on my arm.

"You do?" I asked, not sure I believed him.

He must have heard the disbelief in my voice, because he looked at me with a puzzled expression.

"Yeah, why wouldn't I?"

"I don't know …" I said with a shrug. "I just didn't think you would."

He peered at me quizzically for a minute, then looked me over before a hurt expression crossed his face.

"Is that what all of this has been about?" he asked with a wave of his hand. "The piercing, the hair, and now the tattoo … Are these all things you've wanted to do, but somehow thought that I wouldn't allow you to do?"

I cleared my throat, uncomfortable, and for some reason suddenly feeling guilty.

"Um … I don't know, I guess," I stammered. "I've always wanted to do these things, but I didn't think you'd like it, so I never did."

"Jesus," Cal exclaimed, running his hands through his hair in frustration. "I want you to do what you want to do … I always have. If you want to tattoo your entire body, shave your head, and dye yourself blue … go for it. I'm not your ruler, Shelly, and I can't believe that you've ever thought that I would dictate what you could or couldn't do."

"It's not like that …" I said, trying to explain, but the hurt radiating off of Cal was palpable, and it suddenly didn't seem like anything I'd say would help.

"It sure as hell seems like that, doesn't it. Is that what you think of me, of the last six years of our relationship?" Cal took a step closer to me, his voice low so as not to broadcast our fight to the entire restaurant. "No wonder you're so quick to give up … I thought we were in a partnership, Shel. I've never expected you to ask my permission to do anything. I *love* you, for who you are, and I want you to do what makes you happy."

My heart pounded loudly in my chest, and I felt a mixture of regret and fear running through me.

"Cal, you're taking this the wrong way. Yes, I've always wanted to do the things I'm doing now, and I didn't because I didn't think you'd like it." His eyes narrowed at that, and I rushed on, hoping to make him understand. "Not because you wanted to dictate what I did or didn't do, but because you liked me so much the way I was that I didn't want to change anything. I wanted you to find me attractive …"

Cal's face smoothed out at my words, and when I was finished, he stepped even closer. Close enough that I could smell the mixture of sweat and grease on his body, and see his chocolate eyes darken as he said, "Never doubt how attractive I find you, Shelly. You were hot as hell before, and you're hot as hell now. There isn't anything that you could do to your appearance to make me not want you. I want you every minute of every day, Shelly. I promise you that."

"Cal, your order's ready," the guy behind the counter shouted out suddenly, causing me to jump.

My heart was beating rapidly and my breath was shallow. When he turned to grab his order, I stood there for a moment, trying to gain my bearings.

"I'll talk to you later," Cal said as he moved passed me toward the door.

"Cal," I said quickly.

He turned and waited for me to say what I wanted.

"Text me about Saturday," I said. He nodded and walked out, leaving me feeling more conflicted than ever.

Chapter 29 – Cal

I stood in Shelly's kitchen … again, waiting for her to finish getting ready. I'd told her to dress up and be ready to go at six, but when I'd arrived she asked me to give her a few more minutes.

I checked my watch, saw that we still had enough time, then glanced around the kitchen. This was the first time I'd been here during the day, and the place had "Shelly" written all over it.

She'd gone with a blue and yellow theme, which made me think of U of M, although I'm sure that wasn't her intent. There were colorful appliances, towels, and yellow flowers in blue-pitcher-style vases. It looked fresh and homey. Shelly had a knack for making a house a home, no matter where she lived.

I sighed as it hit me …. I may not ever live with her again. I probably needed to remove myself from Scott's home and find a place of my own, but I didn't want to. I could be honest with myself and say that above all, I was hoping that after our next three dates, I'd be moving in here with Shelly.

Did that make me optimistic or naïve?

I probably needed to come up with a backup plan. It was time for me to give Scott his space back, and figure out what I was going to do with myself, if Shelly still wanted a divorce when this was done.

After the events of the last week, I had to admit that things weren't looking good for "Team Cal."

I heard the tapping of heels down the hall, and looked up to see Shelly enter the kitchen from the hallway.

Her hair was swept up, leaving her neck exposed. I'd always loved the soft expanse of her neck, and often spent a lot of time there, nuzzling or brushing my lips along the length of it. She was wearing a dress that hit just above the knee and swayed a bit when she walked. It was a halter-style dress, and I'm sure she picked it to show off her new tattoo, the script dark and sexy against her creamy skin.

She looked amazing, from the top of her head to the point of her black heels. My body grew taut with the familiar tug of longing, and I felt comforted in the fact that my wife, even after six years, turned me on like no other woman ever could.

"You look beautiful," I said, walking over and offering my arm to her.

"So do you," she responded with a smile.

It wasn't often that I wore slacks and a tie. I was more of a jeans and T-shirt kind of guy, but the look on Shelly's face as she looked me over was making me think I could become a convert.

"Ready?" I asked.

She picked up her little black purse and nodded.

Once we were settled in the car and en route to date number six, I felt excitement and apprehension. Excitement, because we were about to do something that Shelly had always really wanted to do since she was a little girl, and apprehensive, because we only had two more dates.

Two more Saturdays.

Two more weeks.

I looked over at Shelly's profile as I drove, trying to take her in and memorize how she looked in this moment.

I honestly didn't know what my life looked like without her in it, and I didn't want to.

"So … Where are we going?" Shelly asked with a grin.

I shook my head and mimicked closing my

lips and locking them with a key, then threw the invisible key to the side, causing Shelly to laugh.

We rode the rest of the way in companionable silence, and when we reached our destination, I slowed down a bit, allowing Shelly to look out the window to see what was written on the bright marquee.

She gasped and squealed, "The ballet?" She turned to me in awe, clapping her hands together like a little girl. "You're taking me to the ballet?"

I nodded, trying to keep a smile on my face, although I expected the next few hours to be more like a jail sentence than something to clap about.

I escorted her inside and to our seats, all the while Shelly chattered excitedly about how she'd always wanted to see the ballet, and had dreamed of being a dancer as a child. I knew all this of course, hence … the jail sentence, but I was really happy at how thrilled she was about this date.

The lights went down and the music began to play. Shelly sat on the edge of her seat, her eyes wide, an expression of utter happiness on her face. I glanced at the dancers on the stage, then turned my focus back on Shelly. I'd rather watch her enjoy the show than suffer through the show itself.

I settled back into my seat, my gaze on my wife's face, watching as it went through a myriad of emotions. Happiness, sadness, awe, and even a little pain. I loved how utterly enthralled she was by the performance.

As the ballet drew on, I began to battle the exhaustion of the day. I'd gone in early to help TJ with an engine repair, and we'd had complications trying to meet the deadline, so I was physically drained. The music lulled me, until the little pink people jumping across the stage became a blur and I fell into darkness.

I heard a giggle and a snort and opened my eyes to blinding light, with Shelly leaning over me and poking my arm.

"Wake up, sleepy-head," she said softly.

I sat up quickly and tried to look alert.

"I wasn't sleeping," I saidhurriedly , trying to get my brain to catch up with what was happening as people began to stand up and file out of the theater.

"Yes you were," Shelly said with a stern look and her finger pointed at me. "You totally fell asleep."

"No," I argued. "I just closed my eyes for a minute.

"Try thirty minutes," she countered, unable to control her smile any longer. "I think you snored."

"I did not," I replied.

Shit, had I fallen asleep for a half an hour?

I looked up at Shelly, worried that she'd be pissed that I'd slept through our date, but she didn't look angry at all. She had the same dreamy expression she'd worn since we pulled up to the theater.

"I'm sorry, I didn't mean to fall asleep."

"That's okay, Cal," Shelly said, her eyes dancing with delight. "I'm so happy you brought me to the ballet. I loved every minute of it, even your snoring." She giggled again at the look on my face.

I felt bad.

"Thank you so much for bringing me. I know it's the last place in the world you want to be."

I lifted my hand and stroked her bottom lip with my thumb, looking into her eyes as I said sincerely, "I want to be wherever you are."

Shelly gasped, her eyes darkening as my thumb continued to caress her. She opened her lips slightly, her tongue flicking out to lick my thumb as it stilled, then said, "Let's get out of here."

Chapter 30 – Shelly

My body felt like it was on fire. On. Fucking. Fire.

Watching the dancers had been sensual and beautiful, but when I'd turned to see that Cal had fallen asleep next to me, I'd been overcome by lust and longing.

He was so handsome in his button up and tie, his hair styled perfectly messy. His face had looked more peaceful than I'd seen in ages, and I'd wanted so badly to lean over and kiss his full lips.

A couple of weeks ago, I'd have done just that. I would have caressed his face and used my tongue to part his lips and wake him up.

I'd felt a pain in my heart as I watched him, knowing how I wanted him, but no longer able to claim him as my own. At least not until I made up my mind as to what our future would be.

When he'd woken up he looked so deliciously

rumpled that I knew I wanted to take him home, but when he'd brought his thumb to my mouth, caressing me softly … That *want* became a furious *need*.

I unlocked my door with shaky hands, then motioned for him to come inside. He walked straight to the kitchen, causing me to frown. I'd wanted to take him into the living room and attack him, but I guessed that I could make the kitchen work.

He stood at the counter, waiting and watching my approach. I slowed a bit, putting an extra swing in my hips, eyeing him appreciatively as I walked. His tie was slightly askew, so I reached up and pulled the knot, loosening it a bit, then using it to pull him to me, my mouth fusing with his.

I kissed him greedily, hungrily, and he met me stroke for stroke, bringing his hands to my hips and pulling me tightly against him. I shifted him, guiding him away from the counter and toward the table, my lips never leaving him, just growing more frantic. I kissed along his jawline and down his neck, inhaling the spicy scent of his cologne and feeling the impact of that scent at my core.

I broke away, quickly grabbing a chair and turning it, then pushed him gently back to make him sit.

He watched me, his eyes dark with need, as I

stood in front of him and turned, keeping my eyes on him. I reached back and slowly pulled my zipper down, watching his eyes follow my hand as it made its descent, exposing skin along the way. I stopped, right above my bottom, and I pulled the fabric apart slowly, his gazing sweeping my naked back as I pulled the sleeves down and let the top of the dress drop, leaving only my bottom half covered.

I widened my stance and began to shimmy out of the dress as I bent slowly at the waist, exposing the satin bikini briefs that barely covered my ass. His hands reached out, caressing my cheeks softly, reverently, causing me to groan at the delicious feel of his hands on me.

I stepped out of the dress and pushed it to the side, then turned, clad only in my heels and panties, before bringing my hands up to my hair.

Cal's eyes focused on my breasts as they lifted with my movement, and I felt completely and totally empowered.

I took the pins and barrettes out of my hair and shook my head, allowing it to fall down around my shoulders. I ran my hair through the thick tresses briefly, hoping to make them look tousled and sexy, rather than crazy and out of control.

I stepped closer, reaching my hands out to unbutton his shirt. He watched me, not moving to help me undress him, but leaving me totally in control, as if he could tell that's what I needed.

I pulled his tie over his head and pushed the shirt off of his shoulders. He let it fall and lay bunched on the chair, and I reached for his pants. He lifted his bottom for me, so I could pull the pants down his leg. When my bare breasts brushed his legs, he let out a hiss that I felt to the bottom of my toes. My body was tense and yearning, eager for release, as I fumbled with the tie on his dress shoes. When the knot didn't want to come undone, I pulled the shoes off roughly, then yanked his pants off and stood.

I straddled him, both of us naked except for our underwear, and leaned in, trailing kisses up his chest and neck, brushing my breasts along him as I moved. When I reached his lips, I paused, just a breath away from touching him, and brought my eyes to his. He looked deeply into me. I licked my lips slowly, then leaned closer and licked his. There was a second of tension before our control snapped, and we came together with a fury of desire.

I rocked against him as our lips met, trying to ease the painful need that was burning through me. My hands caressed his body, touching, teasing, and scratching softly, as if I was trying to brand every inch of him with my touch.

Cal kept one hand at my hip, as the other traveled up my back and into my hair. He fisted it softly and tugged, causing my head to fall back and expose my neck for his kiss. He kissed and licked along the length of my neck, across my collarbone, and then gently licked the script of my tattoo. I watched through heavy eyes as his head came back, then dipped lower, and his mouth found my nipple.

I moaned loudly and rocked harder, feeling his cock thicken and grow with every thrust. I felt the overwhelming need to have him inside me.

Now.

I reached between us and opened the flap in his underwear, so his cock sprang free. I stroked it, running my thumb along the tip and growing hotter as Cal groaned against my breast.

I quickly moved my panties to the side, stood on my tiptoes, and slid him into me as I sat back on his lap. We stilled for a moment as I stretched and became adjusted to the length of him inside me, then I brought my gaze to his and began to move. Slowly at first …

He brought both hands to my hips and helped guide me up and down. My breath hitched and I closed my eyes, letting the sensations take over.

It felt so good … I never wanted it to end.

I felt one of his hands come to my breasts, and

I moaned louder as he pinched my nipples between his fingers.

I began to ride him harder, then slowly pulled myself up the length of him before slamming back down to ride him again. I watched Cal's face, and as his eyes became heavy and his breath became shallow, I felt the orgasm rip through me.

I rode it out, my body spasming and contracting around him, and I smiled triumphantly when I heard Cal shout out with his own release. His hands back on my hips, he rocked me gently, milking out the last of his orgasm, and I let my head fall to his shoulder. When we were both still, I sighed contently and softly licked the base of Cal's neck. I loved the salty taste of him, and the sound of his heavy breathing in my ear.

After a few minutes, our breathing evened out, and I began to feel my legs getting stiff.

I leaned back slowly and looked at Cal with a smile.

"I'm gonna go clean up," I said, not really in any hurry to move, my body soft and pliant.

"Can I stay?" Cal asked his gaze intent on my face.

I felt my body begin to tense with the knowledge that my response was not going to be what he wanted to hear. I wasn't prepared to spend the night with him.

I shook my head sadly, "I'm not ready for that."

I felt the hurt on his face, as much as I'd ever felt my own.

"So … You can have sex with me, but you won't let me hold you?" Cal asked, shifting so that I had to stand up or fall off.

He stood as well and reached for his pants.

"Is this some kind of payback?" he asked gruffly.

I shook my head. It wasn't … was it?

No, as much as I felt betrayed by him, I'd never withhold my love as a means of revenge.

"Cal, it's not like that. I'm just not ready to have you sleep over. I don't know what I'm going to do, and I don't want to let you in, only to hurt you more in the end."

"Shit, Shelly, you think this doesn't hurt? It's going to hurt whether you let me sleep over or not. You can't keep running hot and cold. You can't fucking strip in front of me and let me have your body, but keep your heart out of it." He dressed quickly and looked at me in sorrow. "You. Are. My. Wife. I. Am. Your. Husband."

I felt his distress, but I couldn't spend the night in his arms, snuggling and sleeping together as if nothing had happened. I wasn't emotionally ready for that yet.

"I'm sorry," I said, my eyes beginning to fill. "I can't give you what you want right now."

I picked up my clothes and ran back to my bedroom. I cleaned myself up and washed my face before putting on my pajamas and walking back into the kitchen.

I walked in and looked around with a heavy heart. Cal was gone, and everything was put back in its place, as if nothing had ever happened.

Chapter 31 – Cal

I hadn't spoken to Shelly all week, other than to text her to let her know that I would pick her up the next night and that she could just dress casually. She'd responded with an "OK" and that was it.

I wasn't sure how we were going to react when we saw each other again; we'd left things pretty badly after our last date.

The sex had been amazing.

Absolutely amazing.

But I couldn't help feeling used and hurt after everything we'd said. I'd thought about canceling our date, but I didn't want to miss out on the opportunity to be with Shelly, no matter how hard it was.

"Are you gonna play, or are sit there and stare at the wall all night?" TJ asked, pulling me out of my thoughts.

We were hanging out at Scott's house. Me,

Scott, TJ, and Craig. We'd thought we could all use a guy's night, so we'd gathered here on a Friday night to play Euchre and talk sports.

Of course, no matter how much we said we were going to just talk sports, the conversation always made its way back to women.

"So, even though you screwed up royally, you still managed to get back in to Shelly's pants … again," TJ said with a grin. "I swear, you're the luckiest son of a bitch I know."

"Shut the fuck up, TJ," I replied with a scowl.

"I can't believe you were such an asshole." This came from my little brother, who drank from his beer and looked at me, his face full of anger.

I'd finally told him what was going on with me and Shelly, and he'd been just as pissed off as I'd thought he'd be. He'd loved Shelly from the moment I brought her home, and I knew he'd hate me for betraying her the way I did. When it came down to a choice between me and Shelly, I had a feeling my brother would pick Shelly every time. Especially, when the issue was one hundred percent my fault.

"Give him a break, Craig," Scott said, coming to my defense. Whereas my own brother would side with my wife, I knew Scott would defend me no matter what. "He told you how the shit went down. He didn't set out to hurt Shelly and fuck up his marriage, it was all a horrible mistake. He's been paying the price for the past seven weeks, and he's trying his best to make it up to her. He doesn't need your shit, so either put your man pants on, or put down that beer and I'll get you a glass of milk."

Craig blinked a few times, shocked at Scott's heated defense of me and the situation, because although we'd been living through this for the past few weeks, he'd only just learned about it today. I felt sorry for my brother. He was young and quick to judge, but I knew he was only reacting out of love for my wife. I couldn't blame him for that.

"It's alright, bro," I said to Scott. "I get where he's coming from."

"Are we gonna play cards or what?" TJ asked, trying to break the tension. "If you want to talk about pussy, I can tell you all a tale about a couple of besties I met at the bar the other night ... Talk about a wild night."

TJ chuckled at the look of shock on Craig's face, and I had to laugh at my friend. He sure knew how to change the subject and keep people on their toes.

"You're an idiot," Scott said with a grimace as he shuffled the cards. "You're gonna end up with every disease in the book."

"I'd rather have my dick fall off than be led

around the balls by some chick," TJ countered.

Scott shook his head and said, "About that …
I've been having doubts."

"Doubts?" I asked, sharing a look with TJ
before focusing back on Scott. "About Victoria?"

"Yeah," Scott said, putting the cards back on
the table. He ran his hand over his face, before
turning his bleak eyes on me. "I don't know if I can
do it … Marry her."

I tried to keep my voice calm and not express
the exhilaration I felt at his words. I'd been waiting
for him to realize what a fucking nightmare Victoria
was since I met her. When he'd asked her to marry
him, I'd thought all hope was lost.

"Did something happen?"

"Not anything specific, it's just … everything.
I don't know if I can live with her for the rest of my
life. I don't know if I'm in love with her anymore."
Scott looked conflicted, and as much as I hated to
think of him hurting now, I knew he would be
miserable in the long run if he married her. "She's
been kind of crazy since we started this whole
wedding thing, and I've been starting to think …
Maybe I don't ever want to get married. I like my
place. I like my job. I like making decisions based on
what I want, and not having to worry about anyone
else's feelings."

"I hear that," TJ said as he took a pull of his beer.

"Being married is great, Scott, if you marry the right woman," I said, not wanting him to give up on marriage, but not trying to talk him into marrying Victoria either. "But I do agree that marriage to Victoria would be a mistake … for you. I want you to be happy, and I don't think she's the woman to do it."

Scott hung his head in his hands and said, "Not all women are like Shelly, Cal … You're the luckiest fucker on the planet. And to share what the two of you have … that's very rare. I don't think I'll ever find someone like that, and I *know* that I'll never have that with Victoria. She's too much like my mother."

"It's about time you fucking realized that," TJ said. "I didn't think you were ever going to see it. I seriously didn't know if I could even come to your wedding. I love you too much to see you tied down to a bitch like that."

Scott looked between TJ and me, while Craig just took everything in silently.

"How long have you both felt this way?" He asked.

"Since you introduced us to her," I admitted.

TJ nodded in concurrence.

207

"Why the fuck didn't you ever say anything?" Scott asked. "I mean, I knew you all didn't necessarily get along like we do with the girls, but I figured that's just because you didn't know her well enough."

"I think we knew her well enough to see that she wasn't a good fit for you, and that you *would* end up in a marriage like your parents'," I replied. "We didn't say anything because you loved her. You proposed to her. If we tried to talk you out of it, or told you how we really felt about her, we worried that you would chose her ... That we'd lose you."

I felt like such a girl saying that out loud, but it was true. I'd rather live the rest of my life with Victoria in it than without Scott, and I knew TJ felt the same way.

"We love you, bro, and we just want you to be happy. We'll support you no matter what," TJ added.

"I get it ... and thanks," Scott responded. "But next time ... tell me the truth before I ruin my fucking life."

I chuckled and slapped Scott on the back, "Will do, brother."

"Are we gonna play cards now, or continue to sit around like a bunch of girls and talk about our feelings?" TJ asked with a grin, and I knew he was just as relieved as I was that Scott had come to his senses before it was too late.

Chapter 32 – Shelly

I checked the clock on my phone as I rushed through the grocery store. I was running late. It had been a horrendous day from the get-go, and I'd been called in to work to deal with some issues they'd had with my subordinate's loan paperwork. Now I was rushing to pick up the items on my shopping list so I could get home before Cal came to pick me up for our date. I could've just gone straight home and came back to the grocery store in the morning, but coffee was one of the items on my list, and there was no way I could start my day without it. When we were living together, Cal had always made sure I had a cupboard stocked with coffee, filters, and the French vanilla creamer that I liked.

I found that I missed the little things like that that Cal used to do for me, like keeping my coffee stocked, and filling up my tank. Things I never really noticed … until they were gone.

As I half walked/half jogged toward the dairy aisle, I was taken off-guard when Melody Cannon stepped out in front of me, almost causing me to barrel her down in the middle of the store.

"Hey, Shelly," Melody said slowly, her voice laced with something that sounded like a cross between derision and pity.

It put my defenses up immediately.

"Hey, Melody," I replied. "I'm kind of in a hurry." I tried to walk past her, but she stepped in front of me, blocking my path.

"Oh? Got a hot date?" Melody asked. "Someone from the office perhaps?"

I narrowed my eyes at her and thought back to Carlos asking me out. But, there was no way she could know about that, and it made me wonder why she was asking.

"What's it to you?" I asked her somewhat snarkily. I'd never liked Melody, and I certainly didn't want her in my business.

"Nothing," she responded with a saccharine smile. She twirled a lock of hair around her finger and looked at me innocently. "Just wanted to check in and make sure you were doing okay. What with Cal cheating on you, and your pending divorce … I'm just worried about you is all. I wanted to make sure that you're coping okay, and … you know, getting back on the horse so to speak."

I wanted to slap the gum out of her mouth.

"Don't worry about me, Melody," I said with a grimace. "And don't believe everything you hear either. In fact, I'm meeting Cal in a few minutes, that's why I'm in such a hurry. See ya."

I stayed long enough to see the sweet look she'd held dissolve into the more apt look of jealousy. She'd always been jealous where Sasha, Gaby, and I'd been concerned.

Forgetting her as soon as I walked away, I hurried off to finish my shopping.

I pulled up next to Cal's Mustang in the driveway and grabbed my bags out of the car.

"Sorry I'm late," I said quickly as I rushed around the car when he got out of his. "I'll only be a minute."

"No problem," Cal answered. "I just got here myself."

I left the door open and ran to the kitchen, putting things away quickly. Cal walked in as I was putting the coffee in the cupboard and I said, "Make yourself comfortable, I'll just be a minute."

I ran back to my room and into the bathroom to freshen up. As I put on deodorant and got out my toothbrush, I hoped that things between Cal and I wouldn't be awkward tonight. I knew I hurt him last

Saturday when I wouldn't let him stay ... Again.

And I knew he felt like I had used him for sex ... twice, and I guess I had. But I also knew that if I chose to walk away at the end of all of this, Cal would be hurt that much more if I let him get too close, and as much as he'd hurt me by sleeping with that stupid bimbo in Vegas, I didn't have it in me to hurt him anymore.

We'd already been through enough.

Tonight I was going to go on this date, and I WAS NOT going to have sex with Cal. No matter how badly I wanted to. I had a lot to think about over the next week, and I didn't want to confuse things any more than they were.

I wanted to have a nice time tonight, relax, and not think about what lay ahead.

I gave myself one last look over in the mirror, then headed out to where Cal was waiting. He was leaning up against the counter, looking at his phone, when I walked in.

"Ready?" I asked.

"Ready," he answered, pushing back up off of the counter.

We drove in silence, and I thought over everything that had happened in the last eight weeks. It was pretty overwhelming. There had been tons of emotions, some good, most bad, and it seemed like a lifetime had passed since he'd come home from Vegas. That night, I never would have believed that we'd be where we are now. I was so certain that I would never be able to forgive what Cal had done, not only to me, but to our marriage. Yet, here we were, on date number seven, and the choice was not as easy as it had once seemed.

When the car stopped moving, I looked around, confused. I had been so caught up in my own thoughts that I hadn't been paying attention to where we were going. I looked around the parking garage for clues, but it looked like any parking garage in the city.

"Where are we?" I asked as he took the key out of the ignition.

"The observatory," Cal responded.

The observatory.

Cal had brought me here during our senior year of high school. We'd watched in silence as the different constellations were pointed out, and I'd been amazed at the vastness of the universe. It had been a magical night, and afterwards, rather than going home, we'd went and parked at a nearby lake. Cal had brought along a blanket and we'd spread it out on the grass by the water, and looked up at the stars, trying to find the constellations on our own. We'd lost our virginity to each other that night.

Under the stars, on that black-and-red blanket.

His expression was blank as we got out of the car, but I knew he had to be remembering that night. It was one of the best nights of my life, and I was sure that him bringing me here on our seventh date was no accident. He wanted me to remember our history, and the love that we shared.

We walked to the entrance, but Cal stopped before we could walk inside.

"Let's just enjoy the night," he began. "I don't want to talk about last Saturday, or what you're going to decide after next week. Let's just look at the stars and enjoy being together … Is that okay with you?"

I nodded with a smile. "That sounds perfect."

And that was what we did.

We walked around, looking in telescopes and listening to experts talk about what we were seeing. We stopped in an open viewing area and sat, looking up and holding hands. It was a peaceful and magical evening.

There was no pressure, and no angst. We allowed ourselves to enjoy each other's company, learn a bit, and remember simpler times.

It was a perfect night.

And when he took me back to my house, Cal leaned over and kissed me softly on the lips, then stayed in his car until I let myself inside my house, before driving off into the night.

Chapter 33 – Cal

I wiped my hands on my pants, my nerves causing my hands to sweat and my stomach to churn as I stood waiting on Shelly's father's stoop. I hadn't seen or talked to him since Shelly had moved out of our house and into his, and probably a few weeks before that. I knew he likely wasn't going to be too receptive to my being here, considering the fact that Shelly left me because I cheated on her, but I felt like I had to meet with him and assure him that I loved his daughter.

When the door opened, I looked up nervously and met Shelly's father's curious gaze. He opened the screen door and said, "Cal."

"Hey, Dad…err, Chuck," I amended, no longer sure I had the right to call him Dad. "Can I talk to you for a minute?"

"Yeah, come on in." He stood off to the side to allow me to pass. When I did he said, "And, son, you can always call me Dad."

And just like that, my fear turned to relief.

I walked into the living room and sat down on the couch, waiting for him to sit in his chair before looking him in the eye.

Shelly's father and I had always had an amazing relationship; well, once we got over the initial dating phase and he realized that I truly loved his daughter. Being a single father, he was understandably protective of Shelly, and I'd always respected the job he'd done raising her on his own.

"I'm sorry I haven't been by to see you before now," I began, wringing my hands in my lap as I tried to work through everything I wanted to say to the man who'd been like a second father to me. "At first I was too ashamed, and then I was simply too embarrassed. I betrayed Shelly, but I also let you and my family down, and I'm truly sorry for that. I know you expected more of me... To treat your daughter with dignity and respect, and I failed at that, but I promise you it was never my intent. I love Shelly, I always will, and I've been doing everything I can to try and convince her of that."

Chuck settled back into his chair and looked at me thoughtfully.

"I'll admit when Shelly first came home that night, devastated, I wanted to string you up by your balls for what you'd done, but after she calmed down and explained things I settled down a bit. I still wanted to hurt you, but a little less maniacally. Once she told me that she wanted a divorce, but you convinced her to go on these dates with you, so you can prove her that you belong together, I realized that you were still the boy who loved my daughter implicitly."

I nodded my agreement, eager for him to understand that I was still that guy.

"I don't know if you've convinced Shelly not to go through with the divorce; my girl can be stubborn when she sets her mind to things, but I do believe that you're doing everything you can, and no matter the outcome, you can be confident that you have," he paused and leaned forward, settling his arms on his knees. "When my Gina passed away, leaving me with a toddler and no experience in raising little girls, I didn't know how I was going to manage. But, somehow, Shelly and I figured it out, and I couldn't be prouder of the woman she's become. You had a part in helping her grow into who she is today, and I'll always be grateful to you for loving her the way you do, but, Cal, if she decides that she can't forgive you and she wants that divorce, you're going to have to let her go."

I felt sick at the thought, and as much as didn't

want to believe that divorce was going to be Shelly's final decision, I wasn't a fool enough to realize it was a strong possibility.

"Yes, sir, I understand that, and as much as I'd hate to let her go, I will. I want her to be happy, and if she can't be happy with me, I'll walk away."

Chuck nodded, his eyes sad.

"I never thought the two of you would be in this place, son, I have to admit… But everyone makes mistakes. It's what we learn from them, and how we change, that determines the people that we become. You'll be fine, Cal, no matter what happens."

"Yes, sir," I said as I stood, my nerves back in full force. "I'm not giving up yet though. I came here today, not just to apologize to you, but to let you know that for our last date, I plan to recreate my proposal to Shelly. I love her and, over the past few weeks, I've done everything I could to show her what our future could look like. Now I want her to know that I'm recommitting myself to her and this marriage, that she can trust me, and that I will spend the rest of my days proving it to her."

Chuck stood and clapped his hand on my shoulder, leaving it there as he said, "That sounds perfect, son."

I looked the older man in the eye and gave him my first real smile since I'd arrived.

"I'd like to ask you for her hand in marriage, just like I did before I proposed the first time," I said sincerely. "I promise to spend the rest of my life making your daughter happy."

He grinned back at me, and I was taken back to that life-changing night, over six years ago, when we stood in this very spot. "There is no other man that I would trust with my daughter as much as I trust you, Cal. You have my blessing."

Then he pulled me into his arms and held me tightly.

Chapter 34 – Shelly

I sat at my desk, barely hearing the soft music of Hunter Hayes coming from my speakers as I drifted off into a daydream about being at the concert with Cal. The last few weeks had been amazing, and I had to admit that I was impressed by the dates he had planned so far. I was eager to see what he would pick for our final date this weekend.

I couldn't believe that it had been eight weeks already. Eight weeks since that horrible night that changed everything about our relationship.

I still didn't know what I was going to do. I appreciated the effort that Cal had put into winning me over, and I knew that I did still love him; I just wasn't a hundred percent sure that I could forgive and forget what he'd done. And if I wasn't one hundred percent, there was no way that I could spend the rest of my life with him.

It was scary to think of my life without Cal.

He'd done way more for me than just keep my gas tank full and my coffee stocked. He'd always been my partner in the truest sense of the word, and being apart from him over the past few weeks had really helped me realize that. I missed the way he'd buy my favorite snacks every time he went to the store, sometimes stopping by my office and leaving them on my desk, so I'd walk in to a sweet surprise. He's also kept a secret stash of chocolate at the shop for whenever I stopped by to see him.

I missed meeting him for lunch, and planning out special meals for us to try together. I missed hanging out with our friends, the group of us enjoying a drink or playing games together. Most of all I missed talking to him every night before I went to bed. We used to just lay in bed, talking about our hopes and dreams before drifting off to sleep.

As much as I loved Sasha and Gaby, Cal had been my best friend for the past eight years. I hated to imagine the rest of my life without him.

"Shelly?" I looked up to see Carlos hovering outside my door. Things had been pretty awkward between us since I'd turned him down, and I hoped we'd be able to move past it soon.

"Yes?" I asked with a smile, hoping to ease the tension a bit.

"Um, someone is here to see you. He asked me

to come back and see if you had a minute," Carlos replied.

"Oh, yes. Please send him back," I responded, curious about who my visitor could be. I wasn't expecting anyone today. "Thanks, Carlos."

A few minutes later I grinned broadly, when Craig poked his head around the corner.

"Hey, Shel, I hope it's okay for me to stop by," he said sheepishly as I stood up and rounded my desk to give him a hug.

"Of course it is," I said, genuinely happy to see him. "You can come by any time. I'm surprised to see you though," I said with a glance to the clock on the wall. "Shouldn't you be in school?"

"I'm on lunch. I only have a couple minutes," he replied as I guided him to the chair in front of my desk.

We sat there for a moment, and when I realized he wasn't going to say anything without encouragement I asked, "So … what brought you by?"

He flushed and looked down at his hands, before bringing his eyes up to meet mine.

"There's this girl …"

"Oh goody," I said with a grin, leaning forward on my desk and clapping my hands together. "What's she like?"

"She's cool. She likes poetry and art and stuff. She's nothing like the girls that hang out at my baseball games; she couldn't care less about that stuff."

"What's the problem?" I asked. Craig was a catch, and I was sure I wasn't being biased; any girl in her right mind would be excited to catch his attention. "Have you asked her out?"

Craig ran his hands through his hair, his face baffled.

"She said no."

I tried not to laugh at his shock over a girl telling him no, but he was beyond adorable.

"Don't give up," I encouraged. "You said she isn't like other girls, so you can't expect her to throw herself at your feet just because you asked her out. If you really want to go out with her, you may have to work a little harder."

"How do I do that?"

"I don't know … Pay attention to what she likes to do, maybe show up at a place that she likes to go. You said she likes poetry and art. See if there are any open mic nights, or talk to her friends and see if she likes museums. Do a little research and show her that you are interested in who she is and what she likes," I suggested.

Craig nodded, his face breaking into a sunny

smile. He looked so much like Cal at that age, it made my heart clench.

"Okay, I can do that. Thanks, Shel."

"Anytime, really. And let me know what happens!"

He stood up, so I got up and went around the desk to pull him into a quick hug before he left.

"Hey, Shel?" he asked before walking out.

"Yeah?"

"I know that you have to make a decision that's going to work for you, but I really hope you give Cal another shot. And if you don't, I hope you'll still see us as your family."

Touched, I brought my hands up to Craig's face and promised, "You'll always be my family."

Chapter 35 – Cal

"Thank you all so much for coming," I said to the gang after the last person, Sasha of course, had arrived.

"Of course," Gaby and Scott said simultaneously.

"What's up?" TJ asked.

While Sasha just raised her perfectly manicured eyebrow at me.

I looked at all of them, my best friends, seated around the garage and watching me expectantly.

"As all of you know, this Saturday is date number eight. It's my last chance to convince Shelly that she should trust me, forgive me, and continue to spend the rest of her life with me. If I fail, she is going to file for divorce. That's a fact. Hell, she would have divorced me eight weeks ago if I hadn't convinced her to agree to my plan. As promised, if that's what she decides, I'll sign the papers willingly

But … I'm going to do whatever I can to make sure that doesn't happen."

"What are you going to do?" Gaby asked, sadness taking over her pretty face.

"That's why I've called you all here, just like I did six and a half years ago …"

"Are you serious?" This came from Sasha, by far the most cynical of the group.

I nodded and looked around the room at my friends, as what I'm asking begins to register with all of them.

Six and a half years ago, we were all seniors in high school, but even then, I knew that Shelly was the girl that I wanted to spend the rest of my life with. I began to plan my proposal for the night of our graduation, and I enlisted all of our friends to help me make it as special as possible.

Sasha had been in charge of dressing Shelly, because I figured she'd want to look her best for the night of her engagement. Sasha had taken her shopping for a graduation outfit, and had ensured that she looked amazing for the night that was to come.

Scott and Gaby had been in charge of turning the roof of our gymnasium into a magical place. They'd covered it in twinkling lights, flowers, and candles, and had made it more beautiful than I ever could have imagined it.

TJ had been in charge of getting Shelly to the roof of the gym, where I would be waiting, in the middle of the flowers and twinkling lights, to ask her to marry me.

I still don't know what he'd said to get her up there; that had always been a secret between the two of them that they had refused to divulge, but the end result was still the same … On the evening of our graduation, I had waited in my suit and tie, breathless and nervous, for Shelly to meet me on the roof. She'd opened the door and stepped out, her eyes surveying the area in awe, before landing on me. Her smile had been wide, but puzzled, and she'd walked toward me slowly. When she'd almost reached me, I dropped to my knee and told her all of the reasons why I needed her in my life forever.

We'd cried together, and she said yes. It was the most amazing night of my life, and all of our friends had been there to help us celebrate.

"You want to recreate that night," Scott said. "The night you proposed.

"I do," I replied. "If that doesn't work … Nothing will."

"What if she says no?" Gaby asked softly, her face still wrought with worry. Out of all of our friends, she was the one who took things to heart the most. I knew, if Shelly and I divorced, she would take it the hardest out of all of our friends, and I loved her dearly for it.

"If she says no … I'll deal with it, Gaby. I'll have no choice. She gave me eight weeks, I can't ask for more than that," I answered truthfully. "I'll never stop loving her, but I'll have to move on with my life."

Gaby nodded sadly, a tear running down her cheek. I walked over to her and wiped her face with my palm.

"Happy thoughts, Gabs," I said with a smile. "I'm not going out without a fight."

She took a deep breath and nodded, giving me a watery smile.

I turned and looked at each of my friends in the eyes before asking, "Are you all in?"

"You know it, brother," Scott said. "Gaby and I know where to go and what to get to make the roof look the same as it did that night."

I turned to TJ.

"Yeah, man … I'll get her there. You just let me know what time," TJ said with a grin.

I looked at Sasha, who didn't look convinced.

"What?" she asked. "You want me to take her shopping? What if *this* isn't one of the greatest nights of her life, but rather … one of the worst? Do you really want her to remember it forever?"

"No, Sasha, I don't expect you to help her get dressed up. I couldn't care less what she is wearing, and you're right, this night could go either way ... Really good, or really bad. I just want you to take her out beforehand and get her something nice. Something that will make her happy, regardless of the outcome of the night. As before, I'll give you the money ... I just want you to make sure she's happy. I know that you're still pissed at me, I get it ... But you have to know that I love her, and that I always will, regardless of the dumbass mistake that I made."

I looked deeply into Sasha's eyes, imploring her to believe me, knowing deep down that no matter how disappointed I'd made her, she knew that the love I felt for Shelly was the real thing.

"Okay," Sasha said finally. "What do you want me to get her?"

"I've got just the thing," I responded with a smile.

We spent the rest of the afternoon talking and hanging out. There wasn't much to plan, since we'd already played out this event once before, but it was fun to relive the experience again.

We laughed and joked, stopping to order food and sneak a couple of drinks from the bottle that I kept in the bottom of my toolbox.

It felt great.

Great to have my friends together again, as if the past eight weeks had never happened, and our unit had never been damaged.

"Hey, Sasha," TJ said as he brought a slice of pizza to his mouth. "I heard you went out with Little John from the bar … You must be running out of guys if that's the case."

Little John was a three-hundred-pound bartender with a heart of gold, and a wife who loved him dearly.

"Fuck off, TJ," Sasha replied, her lip curled in derision. "You're just jealous cause little Miss Melody has been sniffing around Cal instead of being infatuated with you. I guess you aren't as great a lay as you think you are."

I cringed at the mention of Melody and her apparent crush, but laughed at the look on TJ's face.

"Shit," TJ responded. "That girl is batshit crazy … But if you're so curious about what I'm like in the sack, Sasha baby, I'd be happy to take one for the team."

Sasha jumped to her feet at that, her red hair flying, and her cheeks splotchy with anger. No one could piss her off like TJ could.

"Take one for the team, my ass," Sasha said, walking toward TJ with an exaggerated shake of her hips. "You know you go to bed at night and dream of me. Wishing that one day I'd take pity on you and show you what it's like to sleep with a real woman … Not just some whore from the bar."

"Alright, guys," Gaby cut in, always the peacekeeper. "We get it … You're both young, hot, and virile. How about you let it go and focus on Cal and Shelly. We need to do whatever we can to help Cal win her back."

I smiled gratefully at Gaby, thought about having another piece of pizza, then realized that I really didn't have much of an appetite. I was too nervous.

I prayed to God that my plan would work, and that after this Saturday, I would be back together with my wife.

I wouldn't stop planning dates though. I'd discovered a lot over the past few weeks, and I realized that our marriage wasn't as solid as I thought it was … Not when Shelly felt she needed my permission to do things that she wanted, and not when there were so many things that we wanted to do, but hadn't made time for.

I promised myself that if she did take me back, that I'd be more cognizant of the little things that made her happy, and that I'd step out of my comfort zone and try new things with her. If the last few weeks had taught me anything, it was that we'd been coasting along in our little bubble, happy and satisfied, but that there was so much more out there that would bring joy to our lives. We just had to get out there and give it a shot.

Chapter 36 – Shelly

I didn't catch on at first … Not when Sasha came by early Saturday morning to take me shopping at Kohl's. Not when she offered to buy me a Keurig, so I'd always have the perfect cup of coffee seconds away. Not when she went through my closet to help me pick out the perfect outfit for my final date with Cal. And not when she hugged me tightly, with tears in her eyes, and told me to keep an open mind, and do what came naturally.

No … I just thought she was as emotional as I was, knowing that this was my final date with Cal.

I caught on when TJ showed up at my door instead of Cal, looking handsome as sin, with a smile just as devilish.

"What are you doing here?" I asked when I opened the door.

"Cal's been injured at the gym playing basketball and he's been calling for you. We have to hurry." He said the words in an over-exaggerated tone of worry, unlike the night of my proposal, when I'd believed him whole-heartedly and had gone racing past him toward the gym.

I stood there and looked at him, my heart both conflicted and buoyant at the same time.

"Really?" I asked, silently asking him to confirm what I thought he was saying.

"Really," TJ said with a small smile, offering his arm to me.

I looked from his face to his arm, then back again.

Cal was going to propose.

Just like he had the night of our high school graduation.

Should I go … and possibly break his heart?

Or should I leave him there, embarrassed in front of our friends, and save myself the emotional turmoil that would come from going?

I took TJ's arm and let him lead me to his car.

We drove to the high school in silence, the events of my last proposal replaying in my head. It had been so romantic, and so unexpected. Everyone had said that our love would never last, that we were too young, but Cal and I hadn't cared. We'd believed, one hundred percent, that our love was true, and that it would last forever.

When we arrived at the school, TJ walked me up the stairs and to the roof of the gymnasium, then stepped to the side as I opened the door.

I was taken back to that night … It looked exactly the same. Lights strung up and twinkling, flowers spread around the roof, filling the night with their beautiful fragrance, and candles flickering in the wind. In the center of it all stood Cal, handsome and proud in his suit, his hair blowing in the breeze, a giant smile on his face. This time, his smile was tinged with worry, but he looked even more handsome than he had that night, six years ago.

I walked slowly toward him, my maxi skirt swaying a bit with every movement, and I stopped a few feet in front of him.

He stepped forward and took my hands in his, squeezing them gently before he began to speak. "Shelly, I know that what I did was unforgiveable, and I won't blame you if you can't see past it and continue on in this marriage with me. I don't know if I'd be able to stand the thought of you being with another man. Honestly … it would kill me, so I get it. I'm betting on the fact that you're a better person than me. You just are … I'm also betting on our love. Shelly, we have both known since the moment we met that what we have is special, and most people are never lucky enough to find a love like ours. I have never wanted another woman the way that I want you, and when I woke up and realized what I'd done, I wanted to die. I knew that it would rip us a part, but I couldn't keep it from you, Shelly. I couldn't lie to you, not about something as important as that, even though I knew you would hate me for it. And you did … I saw it on your face, and felt it in your rejection … You hated me for it."

Cal closed his eyes and squeezed my hands again before taking a deep breath and continuing, "Thank you for giving me these last eight weeks. You didn't have to. You could have served me with divorce papers right then and there, and you would have been totally justified. Thank you for giving me a chance to prove my love to you. I learned a lot over the past eight weeks, not just how much I love you, and always will, but that our marriage wasn't as perfect as I thought it was. Shelly, I never want you to feel like you have to ask me permission to do what you want … I'm your partner, and I want you to view me that way. I want you to feel comfortable enough in your own skin to tell me what you want, and I'll do the same for you. I want to spend the rest of my life learning about you. I want to be surprised by you, and I want to keep trying new things together. We have tried more new things over the past eight weeks than in the six years of our relationship. I want to keep exploring with you, and finding out what we like and don't like. More than anything, I want to be allowed back into your life, every day, and every night. I want you back, Shelly, now and forever, and I want to spend the rest of my life, proving how much I love and cherish you."

I stood immobile as he spoke, everything he said washing over me in waves of emotion. Everything he said was perfect, he was perfect, and yet I was still terrified. Terrified of the thought of life with him, and terrified of the thought of life without him.

I looked around as he waited patiently for me to speak, and smiled at our friends watching and waiting in the sidelines, just as they had the night of our engagement.

But tonight wasn't about our friends … What we'd been through was totally about us, and not about them … So, although I loved them, I didn't feel like sharing this moment, and my decision, with anyone but Cal.

"Come with me," I whispered softly.

His face fell as he realized I wasn't going to respond to his declarations right away, but he nodded and let me lead him off the roof and toward his car.

"TJ drove me," I explained when I walked him

to the Mustang.

He unlocked the door and held it open for me, closing it once I got inside. I knew that I was probably torturing him by not answering him right away, but I needed to respond in my own way.

If the past few weeks had taught me nothing else, they'd taught me to stand up for what I wanted and voice my opinion.

"Can you take me to my place?" I asked.

Cal drove the car out of the parking lot and headed toward my condo. You could cut the tension with a knife, and I almost broke down and put him out of his misery, but I couldn't, not yet. I needed to do this the right way, so there'd never be a question, and there'd never be any regrets.Once we got to my place, I led Cal inside and into the kitchen. His shoulders sagged, and I could tell by the look on his face that he knew I was about to tell him it was over.

I walked over to the table and picked up the packet of legal documents that were sitting on top.

I flashed the divorce papers at him, then looked him dead in the eye.

"This was my plan from the second you told me you cheated on me. I walked out of our home and went to my dad's and I *knew* that I'd never be able to forgive you. Never. But you wouldn't listen, and you came up with this damn eight weeks plan, promising to walk away once the eight weeks were over. Yet here you are … proposing to me as if nothing ever happened."

"Shel," Cal started, stepping toward me with his arm outstretched.

I held up my hand to make him stop.

"No … you had your say, now it's my turn. You pushed me … You pushed me and pulled me until there was nothing left. You took me to do things that I'd always wanted to do, and you showed me how vulnerable and sweet you can be. You accepted me for who I am, never wavering … never losing hope. How am I supposed to fight that? How am I supposed to fight, when the only man I've ever loved is putting his whole heart into keeping me with him? I hate you for cheating on me. I hate the fact that we will never know for sure who that woman is, or if you actually slept with her or not. I hate that there's a possibility that I'm not the only woman you have had sex with, and will have sex with for the rest of your life. I hate that someone else touched you, tasted you, and may have had the pleasure of having you inside them. But … I love you, Cal, and I can't stand the thought of living my life without you in it."

I started to sob, but used every ounce of willpower I had to hold it in, especially when the expression on Cal's face was blinding me with its intensity.

"I don't want anyone else … Only you. I love who you used to be, who you are, and who you will become. I have loved getting to know more about you over the last few weeks, and getting to know more about myself. And as much as I have loved making this condo my own, it will never be home without you in it."

I could tell that Cal wanted to speak, wanted to move, wanted to pull me to him, but I had to get it all out first.

I took the divorce papers and ripped them in two. The sound of the paper being torn was one of the most satisfying sounds I'd ever heard.

"I forgive you, Cal, and I'll forget, because I want you as my partner for the rest of my days."

My hand was still up, telling him to stop, so I dropped it and rushed into his arms.

"I love you," was murmured by both of us as we held each other close.

I don't know how long we stood there, holding each other, but when I pulled away to look into his beautiful face, my heart filled.

I stepped back and held my hand out. "Come to bed?" I asked softly. Cal's face broke out into a huge smile, and he placed his hand in mine. I led him back toward the bedroom, ready to spend the rest of my life in his arms … where I belonged.

Please keep reading for an excerpt of book 2 in the
Time for Love Series, 21 Days.
This is Sasha and TJ's story.

Chapter 1 – TJ

I huddled underneath my covers, quivering uncontrollably, and praying to God that my parents would stop fighting and go to sleep. Fearful that their anger would shift, and they would come looking for me.

"I saw the way you were looking at her," my mother screamed from somewhere down the hallway of our little trailer. "That stupid slut! I could tell you've fucked her."

I heard a crashing sound and willed the bed to swallow me whole.

"You're crazy," my father bellowed, the sounds of glass breaking filled the trailer, and I assumed they'd begun throwing things at each other.

Soon they'd begin hitting each other, and eventually, they would turn their rage on me, or they would make up. Either way, I wouldn't be getting any sleep. I tried my best to start replaying "The Neverending Story" in my head. If I was lucky, I'd lose myself in the world of Bastian and Atreyu, and by the time their story *was over, the house would be quiet.*

"TJ?" the voice of my boss pulled me out of the memory. I shook my head slightly, then brought my eyes to his.

"Yeah? Sorry, boss, I wandered off for a minute," I admitted, slightly embarrassed at being caught drifting off.

"Can you come back into the office for a minute?" He asked, before turning and walking back towards his office, without waiting for my reply.

I looked over at my buddy Cal, who'd popped his head out from under the hood of a Chevy he was working on. He met my gaze and shrugged, indicating that he wasn't sure what the boss wanted this time.

I picked up a rag and made an attempt to wipe the grease off my hands, before proceeding down the hall. I knocked lightly on the open door and peeked my head around the corner.

"Come in and have a seat TJ," my boss said in greeting.

I walked in, running my hand nervously through my hair, not caring that I was probably streaking my dirty blonde hair with grease. Being called in to the office always made me feel like I was a kid getting in trouble again. Or worse, like I was being called in to answer questions about the bruises on my body, when the last time I'd eaten was, or when was the last time I'd bathed and changed clothes. Either way, I hated feeling weak and uneasy.

I sat and waited.

Our hours had already been cut, and I knew business was bad, so I figured whatever the boss wanted to say couldn't be good.

"TJ, you know things have been going downhill here for a while, and I've tried to do what I could to preserve the business and get back on even ground, but I've come to a decision… There's no way easy way to say this, so I'm just gonna rip the band aid," The defeated look on his face made my stomach clench. "I'm selling the business. Mary and I have raised four kids, and I've had this shop for over twenty-five years, and it's just more stress than I want to deal with. We're going to retire and head down to Florida to be by our oldest. She's having her second baby, and Mary wants to be by her grandkids. I know you and Cal will take a hit from this, but you're both hard workers and good at what you do, so I know you won't have any trouble finding another job. I'll be happy to write a letter of recommendation if you need one."

I felt a mixture of anger and hurt at his words. Not because I didn't understand his position, or wish he and his wife the best, but I needed this job. I depended on it. I loved the work, and the privacy of living on the grounds. I'd been picking up painting jobs with my friend Brock's company, but it wasn't full time work, and it didn't pay as much as working at the shop did. The clenching of my stomach turned into a burn.

I hated the thought of losing my job and my apartment. They weren't much, but they were mine. I made a decent living and had a stable environment, something I'd never really had before. The thought of not knowing where my next paycheck was coming from, or whether I'd have money to eat and pay rent, tore me apart.

But that wasn't my boss's problem. It was mine.

I'd start looking for another job and see if I could pick up some extra jobs with Brock.

"When do you need me out of the apartment?" I asked warily.

"This weekend," he responded with a frown. "I'm sorry I can't give you more time, TJ, but we've already had a couple of people interested in the property."

I nodded absently, my mind reeling as I tried to plan what my next step could be. Scott had just gotten Cal off his couch, and he was having issues with his fiancée, Victoria, so I didn't want to impose on him. Cal and Shelly had just worked out their marital problems, and Cal had moved back in with her, so there was no way I would ask them to put me up. Not when they were just getting back on track.

I thought about my grandparents, and felt the familiar rush of sadness. I'd only had them in my life for a few years, but they'd been the best years of my life. They'd taught me what it was to feel loved, and they'd done their best to rebuild my trust and faith in people. They'd passed away last year, so they wouldn't be around to save me this time.

I was going to have to figure this out on my own.

Acknowledgements

Thank you so much to the readers. I can't tell you how much I appreciate the fact that you give my books a chance. Thank you!

Thank you to the wonderful people who agreed to Beta Read 8 Weeks: Marilyn Almodovar, Jennifer Snyder, Kristi Strong, Taneesha Freidus, Autumn from the Autumn Review, Shanyn Day, and Brooklyn Skye. Thank you all so much for your input!

Thanks to Shanyn again, and Inkslinger PR, for the encouragement and support. I love you guys!

Thanks to Kristina Circelli for editing, Kelsey Kukal-Keeton for the wonderful portfolio of photos (I'm so happy with the picture I chose), to Karen at White Hot Formatting, and to the scrumptious Allie at B Design for the beautiful cover. You have all truly become a team to me, and my books are made better because of all of you!

Thanks to Raine, whether you feel the same or

not, I view you as my partner in crime. I'm so lucky to have "met" you two and a half years ago, and I cherish your input!

Thanks to the fabulous women from my Story 4 Story group, for giving me a safe place to talk, vent, and share thoughts and ideas. I'm so happy to have you all in my life.

Finally, a huge Thank You to my family for allowing me to live my dream, and supporting me every step of the way.

About the Author

Award-Winning Author Bethany Lopez began self-publishing in June 2011. Since then she has published various YA and NA books. She is a lover of romance, family, and friends, and enjoys incorporating those things in what she writes. When she isn't reading or writing, she loves spending time with her husband and children, traveling whenever possible.

Made in the USA
Charleston, SC
18 March 2014

Is eight weeks enough time to earn back

the love of someone you've betrayed...

the only one you've ever loved?

Shelly has been in love with Cal since they started
dating in eleventh grade. Despite everyone saying
that the odds were against them, they got married
after graduation and built a life together. Now, six
years later, she is faced with the ultimate betrayal.
Devastated, her first instinct is to call it quits...

After a drunken binge at his best friends' bachelor
party, Cal betrays the one person who has always
been there for him, his wife, Shelly. Terrified and
realizing she might divorce him, Cal must come up
with a way to prove to her that his love is true...

Cal asks Shelly for eight weeks. Eight weeks to
convince her that their marriage is worth the fight.
Will Shelly be able to trust him again, or will their
marriage end the way many others do when faced
with opposition... In divorce?

ISBN 9781493534166

90000 >

9 781493 534166